A CORNISH AFFAIR

A CORNISH AFFAIR

Cynthia Harrod-Eagles

SEVERN HOUSE

This first hardcover edition published in Great Britain 1996 by
SEVERN HOUSE PUBLISHERS LTD of
9–15 High Street, Sutton, Surrey SM1 1DF.
Previously published in 1977 in paperback format only
under the pseudonym of Emma Woodhouse
and under the title of Romany Magic.
This edition complete with new introduction from the author.

British Library Cataloguing in Publication Data
Harrod-Eagles, Cynthia
  A Cornish affair
  1. English fiction – 20th century
  I. Title
  823.9′14 [F]

  ISBN 0-7278-4962-X

For Joe

Typeset by Hewer Text Composition Services, Edinburgh.
Printed and bound in Great Britain by
Hartnolls Ltd, Bodmin, Cornwall.

AUTHOR'S NOTE

This novel is one of those which first appeared under the pen-name of Emma Woodhouse previously only available in paperback. In re-issuing them in a hardback edition for the first time and under my own name, Severn House have asked me to explain how they came to be written.

From earliest childhood I was always a compulsive writer, though of course I had no idea then that I would ever be able to earn my living by writing. I completed my first full-length children's novel at the age of ten – a harrowing tale of a misunderstood orphan and an untamed pony – and over the next eight years I wrote eight more, but though I regularly sent them off to publishers, none was ever accepted for publication.

At the age of eighteen I went off to university in Scotland, and there wrote my first adult novel. I submitted it to a publisher, but it was rejected, though with a kind and encouraging note that I should keep trying. I had no need of that particular advice – I had already begun a second novel, THE WAITING GAME. It took me some time to complete, but when at last I submitted it for a competition for unpublished writers, my persistence was rewarded: THE WAITING GAME won the 1972 NEL Young Writer's Award.

NEL also took my next novel, SHADOWS ON THE MOUNTAIN; and then another publisher approached me with a commission to write three romances. In those days, publishers believed that a writer had to have a different name for each separate kind of book they wrote, and since the romances would be quite different from my previous two novels, I was asked to choose a pseudonym. At the time I was in the middle of my annual re-reading of the Jane Austen novels, and happened to have got up to *Emma*, so I suggested Emma Woodhouse as a pen-name.

Thus I embarked on my first three commissioned books; but meanwhile I had to earn a living. My husband at that time was at college and not earning, so I was doing a part-time evening job as well as my daytime office job to make ends meet. Add to that the running of a home, and the social life of a newly-married couple, and it didn't leave much time for writing; but when you accept a commission, it is vital that you hand in the work on time. Every spare moment of evenings and weekends found me pounding away at the typewriter. Somehow I did it: the books were delivered by the deadline; and in giving satisfaction in this first contract I paved the way for what was to be my career as a full-time novelist.

As I write this, more than thirty books later, my novel EMILY has just won the RNA Novel of the Year Award for 1993; but in spite of all the recent excitements, I still have a particular fondness for my Emma Woodhouse books. They remind me of those struggling days, and I contemplate with amazement the youthful energy that was needed to produce them while juggling with so many other balls in the air. I am very glad to see them reissued in this handsome Severn House edition, with my own name on the cover, and I hope you will enjoy reading them as much as I enjoyed writing them.

CHAPTER ONE

It was one of those years when the summer comes in instalments, and seems all the finer for it. May and June had been gloriously hot, only to be followed by six or seven weeks of grey, cool, wet weather that set the nation as a whole to despair. Now, in September, the country was once again bathed in sunshine, the rich golden harvest sunshine of an Indian Summer.

Sally Trevose and Jim Gordon had been walking all afternoon along the rambling cliff paths above the village of Pengarth, which was their home. While the tourist industry as a whole had suffered from the soggy August, Pengarth had hardly noticed, for the sort of tourists who came to Pengarth were not the sort to be put out much by a lack of sunshine. The village clung to the side of a precipitous hill, and was little more than a tumble of cottages whose descent from the famous cliff tops ended abruptly at the little harbour, which seemed to have been scooped out of solid rock.

It was certainly picturesque: the neat grey houses with their window boxes full of Cornish geraniums; the narrow winding alleys and cobbled lanes; the harbour and its fishing fleet (which incidentally provided most of the income of Pengarth for the rest of the year); and the fine walks across the cliffs; they were all there, and all tourist attractions. But there was simply no room for such frills as amusement arcades, fish and chip shops, dance halls, Wimpy bars and the like. There wasn't even anywhere to swim unless you went along the coast about five miles; and so there was nothing that you could do in Pengarth that you couldn't do almost equally as well in the rain.

Sally, had she known it, was in the way of being one of the attractions of the place herself. She was Cornish born and bred – her father had been born in Pengarth, as had his father before him, and the Trevose family owned a pottery which was still in existence, owned and run now by Sally's uncle

Fred, who lived in the house next door to the pottery on the harbour front, with Sally's grandmother.

Sally's father had been a fisherman, and was dead now, having drowned while Sally was quite small. Her mother had been the schoolteacher, a very pretty young woman from Torquay who had come to Pengarth to get experience of a small village school and had stayed for good. From her Sally had inherited most of her good looks. She had her mother's glorious red-gold hair, her fair skin lightly dusted with freckles, her slender, athletic figure. From her father she had inherited a kind of Cornish stubbornness which showed in her firm chin, and his bright blue eyes.

Jim was, in the local dialect, a 'furriner', although having been in the village since he was a lad of eight, he was beginning to be accepted now. Jim had first come to Pengarth when his father, a widower doctor, had taken over the vacant prac-tice there. Before that they had lived in London, and Jim had had a hard time at first both to get used to the different life, and to get the other children used to him. At first he had been bullied and ostracized at school, but Sally had taken him under her wing, and being the schoolteacher's daughter she had considerable influence, and had forced the others to accept him. From that time on they had been friends, and had fought each other's battles; and somewhere in the back of their minds had been the thought that one day they would grow up and get married . . .

'What are you smiling at?' Jim asked, breaking into Sally's reverie.

'I was just thinking about us as kids. We always meant to marry when we grew up, but it was always just something that would happen in the future. I can't believe it's really happening at last.'

Jim took her hand and squeezed it. 'You can believe it. You're not having doubts, are you?'

'No.' Sally shook her head and smiled up warmly into the face she knew almost as well as she knew her own. 'It's just that it seems to have galloped up on us so fast.'

'I don't call eleven years very fast . . . still, I know what you mean. And tomorrow, you'll be Mrs Gordon. How will you like that?'

'I'll let you know in ten years' time. How will you like being Mr Trevose?'

'I hadn't thought of that,' Jim laughed. They slowed and stopped automatically as they reached the stone wall that bounded the grounds of the new block of flats called, picturesquely, Smugglers Top. A gate in the stone wall opened onto steps which led down to the entrance door, for the block, being built on the hillside, was below them. Jim had a bachelor flat here, in which he and Sally were to live just at first, until they got a transfer to somewhere bigger. The flats had been built at the same time as the Marine Research Laboratory, which was just over the cliff, about two miles away. The Lab, as it was called locally, had provided a much-needed shot in the arm for Pengarth at a time when a lot of the young people were leaving for bigger towns, because there was no work for them. One of the offshoots of the Lab was Smugglers Top, built to ease the accommodation problem that the influx of new people had caused, and at the time there had been much consternation that the new buildings would spoil the look of the place. It had been designed, however, with great tact, and except for the fact that the grey stone and slates were new and obviously less weather-beaten than the surrounding buildings, it might always have been there.

Jim and Sally stood side by side, gazing down over the roofs of the village. There was a wonderful view from here, right over the harbour and the sea, the dark cliffs and the jagged rocks, and one or two small sails out on the misty horizon. The roof of Smugglers Top was just below them, conspicuous by its lack of lichen, with which all the other roofs were gilded, and perched on the ridge of the roof, almost near enough to be spat on, was a great black-backed gull. He sat ruffling his feathers in the late sun, his head turned so that he could keep an eye on the two humans above him.

'They always look so clean!' Jim said, wonderingly. 'When you think of the rubbish they eat . . .' The gull fixed them with its bright black eye, careful but not really worried – he knew he was safe. 'See how the sun's turned his breast to gold.'

Lower down the town the choughs were bickering amongst the chimneys, but up here the gulls gathered, circling idly above the cliffs and coming in to settle on the higher roofs. A herring gull came down and settled a few feet from the black-back, and sticking his neck out made his strange yarping cry. The black-back took no notice.

Sally was looking at the gulls too, but not from the point of poetry. She was always the more practical of the two.

'There's a lot of them in,' she said with faint anxiety. 'I hope we haven't any dirty weather in store.'

'No sign of it,' Jim said with a nod towards the clear sky. 'Perhaps they're just perching for the night.'

'Maybe,' Sally said doubtfully, 'but why so far in? They usually stick around the harbour in summer.'

'Are you worried?'

'Well, we always do have a gale or two this time of year.'

'Good job you're not wearing a veil tomorrow,' Jim smiled, and pressed her hand. Sally smiled. 'I'm looking forward to seeing you in your wedding dress,' Jim went on. 'I've waited a long time.'

'There was always one thing or another to make us put it off,' Sally said. 'First mother dying, then you going off to university—'

'And you going off to Exeter to be a nurse—'

'And when I came back and started working for your father, you were still away—'

'And when I came back, Dad died.' Jim's face clouded for a moment, for his father's death was still too close for him to feel easy about it. Sally moved closer to him, wanting instinctively to comfort him.

'Two orphans,' she said lightly to call him back to the present. 'It's a good job we've got each other.' Jim put his arm round her and stooped to kiss her hair. Though she was a tall girl, he towered above her, a tall fair giant of a man with a wind-tanned face and sun-bleached hair, for much of the work he did for the Marine Research Institution was out of doors, mainly in boats and along beaches.

'You know, I think there is a bit of a wind getting up. Let's go in and have some tea,' Jim said, and they unlatched the gate and went through, leaving the gull to enjoy the view in peace.

After tea they sat and talked about their future together, sometimes getting up and wandering about the tiny flat, discussing what they would do and where they would put things.

'You know, it's a good thing we haven't got a lot of relations,' Sally said at one point.

'Why?'

'Because we'd have nowhere to put all the presents they'd be bound to buy us.'

'Six electric toasters,' Jim said, laughing.

'Three electric clocks.'

'At least five Water Sets.'

'Bedside lamps – what else? Oh yes, millions of pillow cases and no sheets!'

'We wouldn't want sheets – they'd be doubles and my bed's a single.' They were both suddenly silent at this point, feeling rather shy. Then Sally giggled.

'I hope you don't snore.'

'I'm a perfect gentleman when I'm asleep.'

'I hope you are . . . anyway, it's a good job we're good friends, or we'd never cope with sleeping together in a single bed.'

Jim had become suddenly serious. He took Sally's hand and kissed it.

'Yes, we are good friends, aren't we, Sally? I think we'll have a better chance than most married couples. At least we won't have any of those awful adjustments to make – we know each other pretty well by now.'

Sally looked at him shrewdly. She did know him well, well enough to read behind his words now.

'Who's been trying to put you off marrying me?' she asked him sharply.

'No one—' he began, and then realizing it was no good denying it, he said, 'Well, one of the chaps up at the Lab was saying that we knew each other too well, that it wouldn't work because we're like brother and sister.' He looked at Sally apologetically, and she looked back fiercely at him.

'How mean to tease you like that,' she said. 'I don't know why you don't stand up to them. You would if it was me they were teasing.'

'Well,' said Jim, smiling suddenly, 'that's always been the way, hasn't it? I stuck up for you, and you stuck up for me.'

In the silence that followed Sally noticed a flurry of wind shaking the window panes. She crossed quickly to the window and pulled aside the curtain.

'The wind has got up,' she said. 'I think we're in for a dirty night. It's as black as aces out there.'

Jim joined her and looked out past her shoulder. There was nothing to be seen – clouds had covered the moon.

'Maybe it'll blow itself out by morning,' he said comfortingly. 'Anyway, it isn't far from the house to the church.'

'I'm not worried,' Sally said, and turning to him put her arms round his neck, and lifted her face to be kissed. His warm lips touched hers gently, and then his arms came round her and he kissed her passionately, holding her tightly against him.

'Tomorrow,' he whispered in her ear, 'tomorrow you'll be Mrs Gordon. You'll be my wife. I love you, Sally. I love you, my darling.'

Sally pressed herself against him, almost frightened by the urgency of his words. Naturally they loved each other, but it had been – yes it was true – almost a brother-sister love. Now she felt the beginnings of something else, a bigger, fiercer love, and she was almost afraid, as if it was going to engulf her; and yet, it seemed that Jim was asking for reassurance from her at the same time. Perhaps it was always true, that when one said 'I love you' one really meant 'do you love me?'

'I love you too, Jim,' she said at last, and because that didn't seem enough, she said, 'I'm very happy.'

There was a long pause, and then he said in a more normal voice, 'Are you, my flower?'

'Yes,' she said, and she knew it was all right, because he had called her 'flower'. He only used local expressions when he was very happy.

'I'd better take you home,' he said, letting her go reluctantly.

'You don't need to come down with me,' Sally said, but when they opened the door they discovered that the wind had increased to gale force, and Jim said, 'I'll come with you,' in the kind of voice she never argued with.

CHAPTER TWO

If you came to Pengarth by car, you could get right down to
the harbour, provided you didn't meet anything coming the
other way, for a very winding, narrow lane went from top to
bottom of the town, making wide loops to allow for the
steepness of the hill.

Pedestrians, however, were better provided for: from the
cliff walks, right down to the harbour, ran a narrow alleyway
which twisted and dodged in and out of the houses, whose
top end came out just above Smugglers Top and whose
bottom end ran into the harbour round the corner of the
Trevose Pottery. It might have been made for Sally and Jim,
running as it did almost door to door. Because it went down
by the most direct route, parts of it were so steep that steps
had been cut across it; other parts were simply cobbled, but
the lane as a whole had been called Monks Steps from time
immemorial.

During the '50s, when the tourist industry was reviving
after the war, there had been a perfunctory 'brighten up Pengarth' movement in the hopes of attracting holidaymakers
away from the bigger resorts, and one of the moves had been
to smarten up the Monks Steps to make them a tourist attrac-
tion. Holes had been filled in, some of the steps touched up
with stone and concrete, walls repaired and the like, and the
district council had renamed it 'Smugglers Way' and written
some vague smuggling legends into the holiday brochure. The
idea had come to nothing, and had died a natural death, but
it had had the effect of making some much-needed repairs to
the alleyway. No-one called it 'Smugglers Way'. It had always been Monks Steps, and always would be, but newcomers
to the place were confused sometimes, for wherever the
Monks Steps crossed the road on their separate ways down,
there was a neat, black and white, enamelled street sign saying 'Smugglers Way' on one of the walls of the former.

When Sally and Jim came out of the door at the bottom

14

of Smugglers Top, they were not immediately aware of the force of the wind, but they found out as soon as they turned the corner. Jim staggered with the sudden thrust of it, and Sally, being lighter built, was plucked off her feet and flung back against the wall, pinned there by the gale as firmly as a butterfly on a collector's page.

Jim struggled across to her and shouted in her ear.

'Good job that wall was there, you'd have been halfway to China by now.'

She nodded, not feeling it was worth the effort to answer. Despite its being still summer, the wind was like a flaying knife, having come straight off the sea, and she had on only a cotton frock, which had been plenty for the warm afternoon.

'Shall we go back for a jumper or something?' Jim shouted, but she shook her head, wrapping her arms round herself for warmth.

'It isn't far,' she shouted back with an effort. 'Be more sheltered in the Steps.' Jim nodded, and held out his hand to her. She pulled herself off the wall and hitched herself to him by an arm round his waist. He flung his arm round her head and they struggled forward, weaving like drunks as the gusts of wind pushed them about. It was only a matter of about thirty yards to the place where the lane they were in cut into the Steps, but it seemed like an hour's struggle before they ducked down the narrow alleyway and out of the wind.

In the Steps there was sudden quiet, though they could hear the wind roaring over the top of the houses above them. They stopped, panting, to get their breath back. Sally licked her lips, and grimaced.

'Salt. The sea must be terribly rough. Thank heaven it started before the boats would have gone out. If they'd been caught in this they'd have had it.'

Like her, Jim thought with an inward smile, to think first of all of the Pengarth fishing fleet! She was a true daughter of the town.

'It came so suddenly,' he said. 'I don't understand it.'

'You always get gales at the equinox,' Sally said reasonably, 'but it is rather sudden, I agree.' Then she showed herself truly feminine. 'My hair will be a mess tomorrow.'

'It isn't very late. You could wash it again,' Jim said comfortingly.

'Perhaps. Come on, let's get home.'

The wind was blowing almost at right angles to the Monks Steps, so it was only when they came out of its shelter at the intersections of other roads that they were in danger from the wind, and they made a rapid descent to the harbour. Down there it was more sheltered, for the bulk of the cliff kept off some of the wind, but all the same Sally decided to let herself in by the side door of the Pottery, rather than go round to the front of the house, which would mean emerging into the wind again.

'Have an early night,' Sally said, turning to Jim as they reached the Pottery. 'I shall too.'

'Will you dream about me?' he asked, but she knew he was only joking.

'If you'll dream about me,' she compromised. 'See you tomorrow.'

'Don't be late.'

'As if I would. Goodnight, darling.'

'Goodnight flower. God bless.'

He kissed her briefly, and she watched him turn back up the Steps before letting herself in to the haven of quiet that was the Pottery. It was dark except for one dim light over the main kiln, but that was light enough for someone who knew the place as well as she did to pick her way across to the door on the far side, which opened onto the covered close that ran between the Pottery and the house. A moment later and she was in the kitchen via the back door, and really home.

'That you, Sally?' She heard her grandmother calling from the living-room, but didn't answer as she knew Gran would come in directly, which she did. Granny Trevose was by no means the little grey old lady that her name suggested. She was tall and wiry, still very straight, for she had beautiful posture, and as active as a fifty-year-old, though she was fifteen years older than that. Her hair had gone white only quite recently, and Sally remembered quite clearly when it had been the same dark brown as her father's; Gran wore it in a soft coil on the back of her head, and held her head up

16

as if it were a crown she wore. She had the same brilliant blue eyes as Sally, the same stubborn chin, and was still almost as beautiful as she had been forty years ago, and still almost as vain about it.

'I was hoping you'd get home soon. It's going to get worse before it's better,' Gran said as she came in. She was for ever on the move, always working, almost always talking. 'I was doing the ironing in the sitting-room so I could keep an eye on the fire. It never lights properly the first time, and we'll need it before the night's out. Have you eaten? Has Jim walked you home? You should have brought him in, there was no need for him to go back. Unless you're feeling delicate about having him under the same roof on the night before your wedding. That's only silly superstition, you know.'

'I know,' Sally said briefly. It had to be brief when Gran was talking. 'We had tea,' she went on, knowing from practice which question really wanted an answer, 'but I am a bit hungry. Is there anything handy?'

Gran cocked her head on one side for a moment and regarded her granddaughter carefully. She wanted to know if Sally was happy; she had had her doubts about the marriage, for she felt that Jim was perhaps not sufficiently adventurous and exciting for Sally, and she felt that Sally had too much of her own character to settle down with someone meek and quiet. Still, she was also willing to admit that she didn't know Jim as well as Sally did, and that he looked manly enough, if looks counted for anything.

'Everything all right?' She asked shortly. Sally's frank blue eyes met hers without flinching.

'Yes,' Sally said, and Gran was satisfied, for Sally, like herself, never lied. Gran smiled suddenly, with the same smile that had enslaved more than one man in the past, and said, 'There's some meat pie left over from lunch. That wouldn't take a moment to warm up. Or there's eggs.'

'The pie will be fine. No. I'll do it. You do your ironing.'

'I've finished the ironing. Go in and talk to Fred while I see to it.'

Sally yielded to the pressure, knowing that Gran could never bear to stand by while someone else worked, and with

17

an affectionate smile she went out of the kitchen, saying, 'I'll just go and put on a cardigan. It's turned quite chilly.'

'I should think so, the glass is falling as if the bottom's dropped out,' Gran called after her.

'That you, Sally?' Uncle Fred's voice from the living-room.

'I'll be in in a second,' she called to him, running up the stairs that were almost as steep and crooked as the Monks Steps, and flinging open her bedroom door.

The pleasure had not diminished. There it was, hanging on the wardrobe right opposite the door so she could see it the moment she came in. She walked across the room and put out a hand to touch it, a hand that trembled slightly with excitement.

Her wedding dress. It was so beautiful, it was almost like a dream. It had been her grandmother's wedding dress, had been made for her, had cost a small fortune when it was new, and Gran had kept it for her own daughter to wear one day; but Gran had had only sons.

Four sons, she had had, three of whom were dead now. Uncle Fred was a confirmed bachelor, and Sally's only cousin was a boy, so there was only Sally, and to Sally the dress had come at last. Gran had cried a little when Sally put it on after the alterations had been finished; not from any sadness, but because Sally had looked so beautiful.

'It's right for you,' Gran had said, and Sally had felt that was true. She was much of a build with Gran, and the dress had needed hardly any altering – only the bodice taking in a little, for she was smaller-bosomed than Gran had been. She touched the silky material and thought, tomorrow I'll wear it; I'll put it on in the morning, and then I'll come downstairs, and Uncle Fred will be waiting at the foot of the stairs, and he'll smile, and we'll walk to the church, and Jim will be there, and he'll look at me – she knew exactly how he would look at her, with a kind of wonder, almost surprise, the way he had when he asked her to marry him and she said yes. And then – but she couldn't see any further. Her crystal ball fogged over when she tried to think beyond that moment. It was as if she could not imagine what it would be like to be married to Jim, which was strange, because she had been

18

thinking about being married to him since she was about fourteen, and it had never been difficult before.

A little wind leaked in from the window frame and made the dress flutter slightly, and Sally shivered suddenly and realized that her bare arms were goosey with cold. She pulled off her cotton frock and put on a pair of jeans and a thick jumper, and went out, closing the door behind her on the still white dream of her wedding dress. She ran cheerfully downstairs and into the sitting-room, saying, 'Gosh, it's gone all wintry all of a sudden. I feel quite cold.'

Uncle Fred looked up and smiled as she came in, and laid aside his paper, holding his arms out to her.

'There's my girl!' he exclaimed in satisfaction. 'Come you here, my flower, and give me a cuddle.'

She went across and sat on his knee, and he put his arms round her and she kissed the top of his head where the dark hair was receding from his brow. He would go bald sooner than grey, she thought.

'Had a good day?' she asked him, and he began to tell her the day's events and news, as he usually did if he or she had been away since the morning. She loved him dearly, and he loved her like a father, and the times she spent sitting on his lap talking were the moments most like normal, happy childhood for her. She felt comfortable, and loved, and safe.

Sally went to bed early, and so was sound asleep when the maroon was fired, but a reaction as automatic as instinct woke her, and she was out of bed and reaching for her clothes before she had even opened her eyes. She dragged on jeans, socks, and two jumpers, and headed for the door, pulling her hair back to secure it out of the way with a rubber band.

As she put her hand to the door handle the second maroon sounded – a dull explosion that was very much like a heavy door being slammed some way away – and made her pause for a second. The lifeboat was called out, and Jim was a crew member; that was as far as her thinking went, for she heard outside the hurrying steps of her grandmother and hastened to join her. The two women went downstairs together into the kitchen, where Uncle Fred was seated on a stool, pulling on his thick seaman's socks. He too was a crewman, but only one

19

of the reserves; still he would go down to the launching to help, Sally thought. But as they came into the kitchen he looked up at them over his updrawn knee and said, almost apologetically, 'Charlie Parker's laid up, and both the Browning boys are away.'

He didn't finish the sentence. He didn't need to. At once Gran hurried to the table and began to cut slices of bread and cheese.

'Get out a plastic bag, Sally,' she said, 'to put this in. You don't know what you'll need.'

'I know what I'll need more,' Uncle Fred said. He yanked on his second sock and went off into the other room to return with his metal hip-flask, which he gave a significant tap. 'This might come in useful,' he said, and Sally knew he was trying to be cheerful for her sake, though in her just-woken daze she could not think why, until he said to her gently, 'This is bad luck on you, Sal.'

She stopped short in yanking on her rubber boots, and realized that tomorrow – no, today now – was supposed to be her wedding day. Even if the lifeboat came back in a couple of hours, which wasn't likely, everyone would be too tired, and there would be too much to do, to go to a wedding at eleven. She shrugged slightly, turning her head away.

'It can't be helped,' she said. 'We'll have to put it back a bit.'

Uncle Fred nodded wisely. 'Vicar'll understand.'

'Are you going to the launching?' Gran asked her.

'Yes.'

'Come straight back then. I'll need your help.'

The kitchen door banged open and shut again, and Jim was standing on the mat, dripping from the shiny surfaces of his oilskin and sou'wester.

'Ready?' he asked tersely, looking from Fred to Sally and back.

Gran said, 'Charlie Parker's laid up, and some others. Fred'll be going out.' And suddenly her unshakeable face seemed to shake and dissolve, and she turned abruptly and hurried out of the room.

She's afraid, Sally thought wonderingly. Two of her sons

have died at sea, she's every right to be afraid, but I've never seen it before.

'Come on,' Jim said tersely, and the three of them ducked out quickly into the black, streaming night.

Anchored between the two of them, Sally was in no danger of being blown away as she had been before, but they were going head on against the wind, and it was hard to make any way at all. They bent themselves forward until they were almost horizontal, and the spray soaked their faces and ran, saltily stinging, into their eyes.

After what seemed like an endless time they got across the front of the harbour and into the lee of the cliffs, and the going was easier and they broke into a run, feeling that they had wasted time in a dreadfully irresponsible manner. There was only one place where the lifeboat could be launched on account of the rocks and currents that hemmed in the small bay, and even that place was far from easy, and involved much hard manual labour in winching in again. But Pengarth's lifeboat served an area of many and great hazards, and no-one would have allowed the lifeboat to be moved further up the coast when it meant delay in bringing help to mariners in distress.

Now they were no longer alone on the dark cobbles. Shapes loomed up from many directions, all hurrying with bent heads to the same destination. Outside the lifeboat house the men were gathered, the crew and the helpers, the vicar to add his prayers, some of the women to gather information. The news, the cause of the call, filtered through somehow.

'Swedish boat – Nevins Bank – holed – going down.'

'Helicopter can't take off – sending one up from the Tor – won't be able to help in all this spray.'

'Crewman short – Fred Trevose – still one short – young Billy from the garage.'

'Trevose – wedding – vicar—'

The crew were climbing in now, and Uncle Fred turned to Sally with a kind of desperate cheerfulness.

'We'll be back as soon as we can. I think the wind's dropping a bit.'

Sally could not speak without shouting, because of the wind, so instead she gave him a hug, short but hard, which he returned before he dashed for the boat. Jim was going too, but she could not bring herself to touch him. She felt afraid; afraid that she might disgrace him by asking him not to go. One could not choose whether to let one's man go or not on an errand of this kind; and Gran was right in one respect – she would not have liked a man who didn't go. Yet she was afraid of his concern for her upsetting his resolve, and could only step backwards from him and make a kind of 'go on' gesture to him. He looked, she thought, relieved as he turned away. She watched him jump in and then turn back to reach out a hand for young Billy Watt, the son of the garage owner, who was only sixteen and had never crewed in the lifeboat before. Billy's mother was standing beside Sally, and Sally saw her cross herself as Billy was hauled over the edge of the boat. A flurry of wind-driven spray made Sally close her eyes for a second, and when she opened them again and looked at the boat, she could not tell Jim from any of the other oil-skinned figures.

There was a shout, and the boat slipped like lightning down the slipway and into the sea. She gleamed whitely for a moment and then disappeared in the blackness of the night. There was nothing more to be seen, and Sally turned away to get back to the house. Uncle Fred was right, she thought, the wind is dropping all right; but the damage is done, the seas won't moderate for hours yet.

Inside the house was quiet after the howling wind and seething seas, and orderly movement after the confusion of the storm. The Trevose house, apart from the Anchor two doors up, was the only place near enough and big enough for the survivors and the crew to gather, and so it was customary for everything to be prepared here for the homecoming of the lifeboat. Already preparations were well under way, as they would be in the back parlour of the Anchor. The parish store of blankets had been got out of the kist in the hall and were airing by the fire, along with the various sets of spare clothes supplied by the Seamen's Mission.

Gran was at the stove in the big kitchen preparing a huge cauldron of porridge which would simmer until needed. Later a huge pot of cocoa would likewise be brewed for the warming up of half-frozen seamen. Two wives of crewmen were there helping; the doctor would be along later to see to his preparations, with which Sally would help him. She had been receptionist-nurse to Dr Gordon, Jim's father, and when he had died she had remained in the post for the new doctor, a young man called Alexander who was accepted by the village only because he had been a ship's doctor. Nothing but such a very particular association with the sea would have cleared him in their eyes of the blame of being so very young and so very handsome.

Because of Sally's being the doctor's nurse, it was customary for the injured to be brought to Trevose house, while the uninjured went, mainly, to the Anchor, and Sally therefore had to prepare a reception here for those needing medical treatment. As she began her part of the preparations, Sally thanked heaven for Gran's enormous calm and capability. The other two women chattered as they moved about, and, worst of all, kept exclaiming over Sally's misfortune at having the lifeboat called out on the eve of her wedding.

'You always expect gales this time of year,' was all she could think of by way of a reply, and at any rate it seemed to stop them temporarily, being so unanswerable.

CHAPTER THREE

The worst time was when all the flurry of preparations was over, and there was a pause, with nothing to do but wait. Dr Alexander, with more fortitude, and perhaps more need to be rested, had retired for a couple of hours' sleep, and Gran suggested that Sally do the same.

'Why don't you lie down for a couple of hours? I'll call you as soon as the boat comes in.'

But Sally merely shook her head, too restless inside for this calm counsel.

'Well, we'll have some cocoa, anyway. There's plenty for everybody.'

The two wives had gone home, to return when the boat came back, and they were alone in the big, warm, peaceful kitchen. The wind had dropped to a mere gale, so the quiet was intensified. Gran ladled out two mugs from the huge pot of cocoa on the slow plate, and brought them to the table, and Sally curled her hands round her mug as if glad of the warmth, though it was almost hot in here from the double source of the stove and the fire.

For a while they sat in silence, and then Sally asked suddenly, without looking up, 'Why were you afraid? When we were just going, I mean? You aren't usually afraid, are you?'

'There's no point in being afraid,' Gran said, answering the second question rather than the first. 'Being afraid can't help. You have to let them go. You can only pray while they're away.' Sally thought back to her own thought – you can't choose whether to let your man go or not.

'I remember,' she said slowly, 'I remember Uncle Fred saying one time, there's no use being afraid – if the sea wants you, he'll take you, and that's all there is to it.'

'Well, that's true. And there's one thing – the sea takes them when he wants, but he hardly ever hurts them.' Sally looked at Gran, seeing the familiar calm face, the bright blue eyes fierce; and then, once again, saw that disconcerting

24

shadow pass through them, as if something inside were falling to pieces. 'It's only the women he hurts,' she said.

'Well, why were you afraid this evening?' Sally asked again. She didn't think that she might be being cruel in pressing the point; she felt only that she had to know, for her own sake – as if, if she knew what to be afraid of, she might be able to avoid it.

'I don't know,' Gran said wearily, and then, 'I suppose it was because you looked so much like your mother.'

For a moment she didn't understand, and then she realized what Gran meant. Her father had died that way, going off in the lifeboat one stormy night, to be brought back colder than the sea that had killed him. And Gran must have seen him off in just the same way, with Sally's mother by her side. Déjà vu. Two of Gran's sons the sea had taken – Sally's own father, Tom, and her Uncle Frank, who had drowned when his boat was run into by a tanker, straying from its proper channel in thick fog. The other son, Sally's Uncle Arthur, had died during the war, in the bombing. He was the only one Sally had heard Gran mourn, as though only he had died, the others had simply gone away . . .

Gran smiled suddenly, as if she had caught herself out in a minor sin.

'Don't be fretting, Sally. That's one thing you have to learn when your kin are at sea – how to wait. There's nothing in the world you can do, so learn to wait without fretting. Is everything prepared?'

'Yes,' Sally said automatically.

'Then why don't you go and lie down? Go into the front room and lie down on the couch with a blanket, if you don't want to go up to bed. I'll call you in plenty of time.'

'All right,' Sally said, more to please Gran than because she wanted to. I'll never be able to sleep, she thought, but once she was lying down, wrapped in a blanket, staring into the dancing flames of the living-room fire, she found it surprisingly easy not to think about anything, and fell asleep quite quickly.

She woke suddenly, and not knowing where she was, was frightened, had a sense of nightmare, as when one dreams

25

one has woken up and carries on dreaming. She adjusted her vision at last to find she was staring at the fire, knowing with a draining feeling of relief where she was and that Gran was standing by her.

'The boat's been sighted. She's coming in. They'll be here in about half an hour,' Gran was saying.

'I was dreaming,' Sally said thickly, waking slowly.

'Get up now and have a wash – that will wake you up,' Gran said quickly. She didn't want to hear the dream. In some ways she was very superstitious.

Sally followed her into the kitchen, and standing at the sink she washed herself in very hot water, and at once felt better. Gran went off to wake the doctor, and Sally used some more of the hot water to make a small pot of tea, knowing Dr Alexander would want it. She had some herself when he came down and felt better for it.

It was beginning to get light – at least they would be able to land more easily. It was always a tricky thing getting wounded or exhausted people up in the dark.

'They're coming,' Gran said suddenly, with some kind of perception that neither Sally nor the doctor had, and a moment later the kitchen door was flung open, and the first of the survivors came in, a young blond boy, red-eyed and grey-faced, limping between two villagers. Behind came more men, crew dripping and exhausted, helpers still dry and active.

'Bring them in, that's right,' Gran said, jumping up, full of life now that she could be active again. 'Put the boy down here – hurt his foot has he? That's right, let's get those clothes off. That one's yours, doctor. Ethel, fetch the towels. Come in lads, come in – there's hot cocoa ready for you.'

The kitchen seemed crowded in a moment, and at once filled with a number of familiar, pungent smells, and unfamiliarly hoarse voices. Bits of the story came out here and there, enough to piece together the basic facts. The stricken ship had been a small Swedish cargo vessel, and had struck a part of the shallows aptly named The Coffin. By the time the lifeboat had got there she was on the point of breaking up, and only the fact that the cargo was timber had kept her afloat so long.

The Pengarth lifeboat had been, apparently, the only rescue vessel to come to aid the Swedes, though as Barney Hill, one of the crew, said loudly over the rim of his cocoa mug, 'What with the swell and the spray, there could've been half a dozen ships around and we'd've been none the wiser.'

'Two stretchers comin',' said one of the women standing by the window, and there was a note of anxiety in her voice that Sally's own mind echoed – this was where responsibility fell onto her shoulders, hers and the doctor's, and it was never easy.

'It's young Peter Westernra!' The same woman cried out as the first stretcher came in through the kitchen door, one end borne by the vicar and the other end by the grocer.

'He's gravely injured, I'm afraid, poor lad,' the vicar said.

'Take him through to the living-room,' Sally said, standing aside from the door. As the stretcher went past her she saw the young man's face like blue wax, eyes closed. 'What happened to him?'

'He went down between the two boats,' Barney Hill said, and Sally gave a shudder – she could imagine it.

'Th'old timber ship was rolling about that bad we could hardly get near her.' This was from young Billy Watt, round-eyed with the horror of it. 'Then we gets alongside her, and she gives a sudden dash – and bang! the bows struck, and Peter went over just as she swung back.'

Into the silence that this explanation dropped over the kitchen came the second stretcher, carried by two grey, lined ghosts that Sally recognized at a second glance as being the lifeboat's cox, Spinney Tiverton, and his second in command, a wicked old man known as Frenchy Polwheal, who was probably the best sailor in Cornwall.

The same woman, who seemed to have appointed herself lookout for the rest, gave the news before the stretcher got fairly into the kitchen. Turning to Gran she cried out, 'Why Mildred, it's your Fred.'

Sally's heart turned over with a sickening kind of thud, but before Gran could cross from where she stood, attending the

27

young Swedish boy's wounded foot, Spinney stopped her with two words.

'He's dead.'

Gran gave one cry, that seemed to cut Sally like a blade. She did not move, but stood, staring at Spinney with a kind of pleading look, as if begging him to say it wasn't true. Spinney, anguish lining his face now as well as fatigue, hating having to be the one with the news, went on, 'He went overboard at the same time as young Peter. We didn't notice at first – he went over the other side you see.'

'We went about for him once we knew,' Frenchy said hoarsely.

'But it was too late.'

'Take him through into the parlour,' Gran said, the first words she had spoken, and the two men carried the stretcher across the hall to the parlour, a big, cold room that was never used, except for funerals and weddings. It was across the hall from the living-room, where the fire burned brightly in the grate, where Uncle Fred had sat last night, Sally thought, and held her on his knee. Was it only last night? He had put his arms round her and smiled, happy that she was happy.

The men put the stretcher down on the floor, and turned apologetically to Gran, who had walked with them, to Sally, who had followed, and to the others who were crowding the door. Sally looked at Uncle Fred, but she could not think of that thing on the stretcher as Uncle Fred; it may be his body, but it was not him. Spinney was trying to speak again, his face still corrugated with the anxiety of bad news to be told, and no-one but him to tell it.

'When he went over – when the bows struck, and Fred went overboard,' he swallowed and licked his cracked lips nervously, 'well, we didn't see right away, trying to get Peter up, you see – but your Jim, Sally, he saw, and he dived in after him. That's how we knew, you see, he shouted out as he dived in.'

Sally nodded. 'Where's Jim now?' she asked. 'In the Anchor?'

'Sally, love, we never found him.' Spinney looked at her pleadingly, and she merely stared at him, not understanding.

'We went about and searched, and we picked up Fred, but we couldn't find Jim. I'm sorry, lass.'

In the long silence that followed, Sally felt her mind being drawn out into a thin thread. Everyone in the room was looking at her, every face filled with horror and pity. No-one spoke, and it seemed to her that if anyone had said a word, even let out a breath of pity, she would have shattered there and then into pieces.

At the end of the long silence, Frenchy spoke.

'He wouldn't have lived more'n a minute or two in that sea,' he said, and he meant it kindly; for a wonder, being Frenchy.

Sally looked helplessly at Gran, and she, as always, found strength to cope. She drew herself up an inch taller, set her face into lines of endurance – endurance she would surely need in the days to come – and said, 'The dead can wait awhile. Our duty now is with the living. Sally, you've young Peter Westernra in the living-room, needing attention, and there's plenty to do in the kitchen for everyone.'

Thankfully, everyone moved out quickly to work, and Sally crossed the hall to the living-room, to pick up the threads of duty. The doctor was there with Peter on his stretcher on the table in front of him, taking the clothes off the poor broken body. Only a couple of minutes had passed since they carried Uncle Fred in, Sally realized. It seemed like a lifetime.

'He shouldn't be here, he should be in hospital,' Alexander said, looking up as Sally came in, his eyes blazing with anger and frustration. 'He's in a terrible mess. Broken back, broken ribs, a ruptured kidney, I think – internal haemorrhage. What the hell can you do?'

'What about taking him in in a Landrover?' Sally said, forcing her brain, like a rusty engine, into life. Alexander shook his head.

'He couldn't be moved. It's impossible. He should have been airlifted straight there.'

'Could they have saved him?' she asked. He shook his head again.

'He's too badly hurt. He can't live. All we can do is try to make him comfortable. Come on, give me a hand. We'll give him a blood transfusion for the look of it, but there's nothing anyone can do to save him.'

Between them they set to work to straighten out the mess as much as possible. They fixed him up with padding and strapped him so he couldn't move, and gave him an injection to keep him quiet – it was not likely he would feel any pain – and then prepared for the blood transfusion.

'What group is he?' the doctor asked.

Sally shuffled through the notes – all the crew's medical notes had been brought over in case they were needed, and said, 'He's A positive. So are – let me see – Frenchy, for one, and – um – Charlie Parker. That seems to be all.'

'Better be Charlie then, Frenchy's will be half rum and half sea-water by now,' Alexander said. 'Can you go and find Charlie, quick as you can?'

Sally went out at a run, heading for the Anchor where she knew Charlie would be helping. When she came in the door, Charlie jumped up in alarm, backing off from her as if she were brandishing a knife.

'I know, I know,' he wailed, 'don't think I don't blame myself! If I'd a been there as I should've he'd a never gone out, and it'd never have happened.'

'Now, Charlie,' someone said warningly, and Sally suddenly realized what he was talking about. He's blaming himself, Sally thought, for Uncle Fred and Jim being killed – that's a bit far-fetched. Yet as she thought it she felt, deep inside her, a kind of pain, like the pain of a heavy blow that one cannot feel at first because of the numbness of shock, but one knows one will feel when that numbness wears off.

'Charlie, we need your help up at the house,' she said, surprising herself with the clearness and steadiness of her voice. 'We're going to give young Peter a blood transfusion, and you're the only one with the same blood group.' It was not strictly true, but as she said it she knew she was telling the small lie for Charlie's sake, because, as Gran had shown her, people with a grief need to have something to do, something that has to be done. Charlie bent his head humbly.

'Of course I'll come, Sally. I'd give every drop of blood in my veins if only it could do some good.'

30

'Come on then,' she said, turning away hurriedly. She was afraid someone would ask her something, make her think. As she reached the door, someone – a woman, she didn't know who – called out after her, 'How is the boy?'

Sally thought of him suddenly, and instead of his blue-white face on the table, she saw Jim's, and her throat contracted and she couldn't speak. She could only shake her head, and hurried out.

CHAPTER FOUR

After giving Peter the transfusion, Sally went on with the other things that had to be done, and the morning advanced without being marked. At one point when she passed through the kitchen, one of the women grabbed her, thrust her down into a seat and gave her a bowl of porridge with plenty of sugar.

'Eat that. It will keep you going.'

Sally ate without noticing it, her eyes already wandering across the room after the next thing to be done. The men who could go home and were uninjured had gone now, to get to bed for a long sleep; others were being bedded down here and in the Anchor for a few hours' sleep. The injured and the rescued Swedes were already tucked up in various beds around the house, having all been treated for shock and exposure, and with the care of them and the dressing of smaller injuries, Sally had only time enough to look in at Peter every few minutes, until the morning was quite far advanced.

It was about eleven when, passing through, she saw his eyes were open, and he gave her a faint smile.

'Thirsty' was all he could say.

Sally smiled back and said, 'I'll get you some tea.'

She went to the kitchen and filled a feeding pot with a spout – tea was always on the go at times like this – and came back to the patient, who was on his own now in the sitting-room, the other occupants having been moved to other parts of the house.

Sally propped his head with her hand and fed him the tea slowly until he had had enough. Then she set down the pot and checked his pulse which was slow and steady, though weak.

'How are you feeling?' she asked Peter, whose gentian-blue eyes were watching her every movement.

'I don't feel anything,' Peter said. Likely enough, she thought, with a broken back amongst his injuries. She slid

32

her hand under the covers to check, and found that he had been bleeding again, but not much. A small, slow leak that would leak his life away. 'Just sleepy,' Peter added.

'That'll be the sedative,' Sally said; but she had read it often enough to know how a man bleeding to death would often yawn and yawn like a tired child.

'Why am I all tied up?' Peter asked after a moment. 'I can't move my hand.'

'We had to strap you up so you didn't move. You've a lot of broken bones that might go through something important inside.'

'Are you taking me to hospital?'

'Later perhaps, when you've rested a bit,' Sally said evasively.

Peter looked piercingly at her for a moment, and Sally felt uncomfortably as though he had looked into the back of her head and seen the real answer to his question; but after a brief moment his blue gaze wandered away, opaque as a kitten's, and then closed as the sleepiness overcame him.

Dr Alexander came in and duplicated Sally's movements, checking the pulse and the slowly reddening bandages.

'How's he been?' he asked briefly.

'He took some tea. He's very quiet. He's beginning to wander a bit I think.'

'You'd better stay with him for the time being,' Alexander said. 'Everything else is done, more or less. There'll be an ambulance for the Swedes this afternoon, when they've had a bit of sleep.'

Sally sat in the quiet room beside the sleeping man, and felt quite unreal. Lack of sleep, real physical tiredness, made everything seem far off and strange, but there was too the shock she had sustained, which was not as yet felt, except in the vague idea at the back of her mind that she had forgotten something. She began to drift herself; perhaps she dozed – at any rate, she had the feeling of suddenly coming to when she heard Peter's voice say again, 'Thirsty,' and she reached out for the feeding pot.

He took a couple of mouthfuls, and then said, complainingly, 'It's cold.'

33

'I'll go and get you some fresh,' she said, but he stopped her.

'Don't bother. It's all right.' Sally slid her hand under the blankets again and encountered wetness. The bandages were soaked through, and she got up and went across to the bag in the corner for fresh pads and gauze which she packed over the old bandages.

'There, you'll do,' she said, smiling at Peter.

He looked at her blankly for a while, and she thought perhaps he had gone too far to recognize her, but at last he said in a puzzled voice, 'Shouldn't you be getting ready?'

'What for?' she asked.

'For the wedding. Shouldn't you be getting married today?'

'There won't be any wedding today,' she said gently. 'Jim didn't come back, Peter. He went overboard when you did.'

Peter's eyes wandered away towards the firelight. 'Never thought I'd be on land again,' he said with a small twitch of a smile. 'I thought I'd had it, there and then.' He yawned hugely and half-closed his eyes, and Sally surreptitiously felt his pulse again. 'Jim was all right, though. The other boat picked him up,' Peter said drowsily.

'What boat, Peter?' Sally asked him, curiously.

'The fishing boat,' he murmured. His eyes were closed now. She took his hand and pressed it to keep his attention, but he seemed asleep. After a moment he murmured, '. . . look pretty, Sally,' and that was all.

Alexander came through again, this time with Gran at his heels.

'Any change?' he asked.

'His pulse is thready,' Sally said. Alexander tested it, raised Peter's eyelids, looked again at the bandages.

'Why don't you go and get some sleep, Sally?' Gran asked. 'Someone else can sit with Peter.'

'No,' she said. 'I'll stay with him a while. It can't be much longer.'

Sally sat on in the silent room, hearing nothing but her own breathing and the small sounds of the fire crackling. Peter was quiet, as if asleep. Sally took his hand again and laid her fingers against his pulse: it was very slow, very faint.

Once, he gave a sigh, as a person might in turning over in bed. He died a little while afterwards, quite imperceptibly.

Dr Alexander came in and verified the fact, and then insisted Sally went into the kitchen with him to join the others for lunch.

'You've had nothing all day,' he said.

'I had a bowl of porridge,' Sally said. She sounded dazed. The morning seemed a lifetime ago.

Hardly was lunch over when the ambulance and the police arrived together. The ambulance was to take the Swedes to hospital for proper care and treatment. The police had come from interviewing the lifeboat cox and the vicar, who was always the village's spokesman.

There was little more to be added to the story, and they soon closed their books and went away. Sally helped Alexander supervise the transfer of the men into the ambulance, and its doors were slammed and it drove away.

'And now, I must be about my normal work. You don't need to come to surgery this evening, Sally, but I'll see you on Monday as usual?'

'Yes – thanks – yes, I'll be there.'

'Good.' He suddenly took her hand and pressed it, looking down at her with something like affection, which was unusual, for he was generally considered a cold young man, though a good doctor. 'It's a rum business,' he said gently, and that was his way of saying how sorry he was.

The house was quiet now, though still not their own property, and perhaps that was as well, for she was dropping on her feet now, yet would not have gone to bed had someone not pushed her to it.

'Go on, up those stairs with you,' someone said. 'And take a hot bottle with you – if you can find one – land sakes, everything's got legs today. Oh, here it is. Just stand there a minute young Sally, and I'll have it for you in two twos. There! Off with you, now.'

She went upstairs like her own ghost, and found her bedroom as she had left it in the middle of the night – it seemed a year away – with the bedclothes flung back and the photograph in its frame lying on the floor where it had fallen when

35

she knocked it with her elbow as she jumped out of bed. She left it there, too tired to do anything. It seemed strange to be going to bed in daylight, and when she took off her clothes and got into bed, the bed seemed cold and alien and she shivered – she was glad of the bottle. She hunched herself up round its small local heat, and fell asleep immediately.

She woke on Sunday to the sound of churchbells, and turning her head on her pillow found that her clock had stopped, not having been wound the day before. She had slept like the dead, and for over twelve hours, but she felt curiously unrefreshed. It must be late, she thought, for the sunlight was shining through the drawn curtains. She listened, but there was no sound of movement in the house. Not only that, she noticed, but there was no sound of wind outside. The storm had blown itself out, then.

She jumped out of bed, pulled on her dressing-gown and went to the bathroom. A bath, she thought, might freshen me up. She heard the minute bell while she was in there, and some footsteps along the passage to her room and back – Gran had come to see if she was up, she thought.

The bells stopped, and she relaxed in the hot water until Gran tapped at the door and said, 'Breakfast is ready, Sally. Are you coming down?'

'Okay,' she called back, and reluctantly dragged herself up and finished washing the parts she hadn't done yet. She didn't want to face Gran, afraid of what changes the night may have wrought in that iron figure. She didn't want to face anyone – not even herself, which was why she assiduously avoided looking in the mirror, doing her hair by feel. She pulled on a dress and cardigan, stuck her bare feet into a pair of sandals, and went downstairs.

Someone had done a lot of work while she had been sleeping, for the house was clean and all traces of its occupation the day before had gone. The kitchen was as bright as a new pin, the range alight, and a smell on the air of frying bacon that might gladden almost any heart. Gran was there, sitting at the table, alone.

'Your plate's on the range,' she said as Sally came in. 'Tea?'

36

'Please,' she said. She fetched the plate and sat down opposite Gran, keeping her eyes down, and wishing the seats had been arranged some other way; but they had always sat thus, Gran nearest the range, Sally opposite, and Uncle Fred on the side of the table opposite the window, between them. She busied herself with her plate, and found, to her surprise, that she was ravenously hungry.

'Who did all the cleaning up?' she asked when the silence became unbearable.

'Ethel Camlay and Mrs Briggs from the Fisherman's Arms. They said it was all they could do after what we had done. It was good of them.' Sally merely grunted agreement, still unwilling to look up. 'Ethel made the breakfast, too. She's gone now, gone back to get Ernie's breakfast.'

'What time is it, then? My clock's stopped,' Sally asked.

'Just after seven.'

'That was early service, then. I thought it was late.' She was trying to keep to commonplace remarks, but Gran seemed determined to bring her back to the events of yesterday.

'Peter Westernra's gone. His folks came down last night and took him back with them to Penzance. It was a sad blow for them.'

'Yes,' Sally said. There was a pause, and then Gran said, 'Sally!'

Sally looked up, and Gran stared at her and said nothing. 'What?'

'I just wanted you to look at me,' Gran said. 'I was afraid you'd cut yourself off from me. There's only the two of us now, Sally, and we'll need each other.'

Gran was as upright as ever, her blue eyes as blue as ever, but she looked older this morning: a rock still, but a rock the water broke over instead of against.

'Yes, I know. I suppose I was just – well, putting things off.'

'We have to face up to it. Finish your breakfast, and then we'll get ready for church.'

'Oh dear,' Sally said at the thought of facing the whole village.

'Yes, I'm afraid it won't be easy, especially for you. Not

everyone is tactful, and there'll be plenty of prying eyes looking at you. But we have to go. It's the thanksgiving.'

'Thanksgiving!' Sally said bitterly. 'Thank you for giving us some of our men back alive.'

'Mrs Watt will be giving thanks,' Gran reminded her.

'Yes, I suppose you're right,' Sally said after a moment. 'Can I have some more tea?'

They went to the eight o'clock communion, which was the sailors' and fishermen's service. Normally the women went to a later service with the young children, but today everyone was at the early mass, to give thanks for the rescue from the sea, and for the safe return of their menfolk. Someone who had been up as early as Mrs Briggs and Mrs Camlay had decorated the church with flowers, and enough candles were burning to have incensed the low-churchers, had it been for any other reason than this. The sun shone brightly outside, though it was cool, with a stiff little breeze, and the church was crowded, and Sally could not help being caught up with the communal feeling, at least for the duration of the service.

All the favourite hymns were sung, the men adding a leavening of harmony on alternate verses as was their custom with the hymns they knew really well, like the Old Hundredth, and 'Come, ye faithful, raise the strain'. The vicar's sermon was, naturally, about the shipwreck, a nice mixture of praise for the lifeboat crew, pity for the Swedish vessel, solemnity for the dead, and thanksgiving for the goodness of God as seen throughout the whole business. It was the same sermon as Sally had heard him give after every rescue, and perhaps she was alone in liking it the less for that. The people of Pengarth were conservatives in the true sense of the word, and liked to know what was coming next.

On the whole, it wasn't too bad, even when the vicar mentioned Uncle Fred and Jim, and the heads all turned as if on one string to look at her and Gran with a mixture of curiosity and pity. Gran sat immovable, her perennial turban of brown velvet – her 'churchgoing hat' – seeming to screw her head down firmly onto her shoulders. One felt she would not have turned *her* head to look if St Peter himself had come in at the West door. . . .

It was over, and Sally wanted to hurry out, to avoid the chatterers and sympathizers, but Gran was a stickler for etiquette, and wouldn't be seen to hurry out of church as if she had somewhere more important to be, and so Sally had to walk at her pace, and stitch a brave smile across her face as she inched past the crowded pews.

At the door the vicar took her hand and pressed it for a moment, and said, 'I'll be along to see you later at home. We all have to thank you for everything you have done, especially for poor Peter Westernra, poor lad. We are proud of you here in Pengarth, Sally.'

She murmured something appropriate, and stood aside while Gran spoke to him. He had something private to say to Gran, and Sally saw Gran's cheeks redden and her eyes sparkle briefly with unshed tears. The vicar had known Gran for a long time, had christened all Gran's children and had buried two of them – three, counting Uncle Fred in advance – and, if he lived long enough, would no doubt bury her. She had given everything to the village, and was already somewhat of a matriarchal figure.

At home they made a light lunch for themselves of soup and bread-and-cheese, not wishing to face cooking a proper meal later, and then they had to lay out Uncle Fred, for there had not been enough time the day before to do more than straighten him decently and cover him. He had to be stripped and washed and dressed for the coffin which was to be brought round that evening, and Gran, naturally enough, wanted to get the job out of the way before the vicar came round that afternoon. Sally had, in the course of her profession, laid out corpses before, and it would not have worried her in the least, had it not been Uncle Fred, and had Gran not been there; but of course she could not refuse to help, though she didn't quite see it as Gran did, as a privilege.

As they worked, Gran talked about him. It was rather like the Red-Indian burial ritual where everyone has to think of something good to say about the dead man as they stand round his grave.

'He was always the odd one out of the four, the quiet one. A bit of an artist, really – that's why he took over the Pottery,

I suppose. He used to go and stand in there watching his dad working, hour after hour, quiet as a mouse, while the others were out playing. When he got a bit older, he used to get on well with Frank, used to like to help him with his homework. He always had a feeling for children, animals too, anything that was smaller or weaker than him. His dad used to say he should have been a girl, but he meant it well.

'He never used to go off after the girls with Tommy – your dad – Arthur was gone by then, of course. He was too shy. He never had two words to say to a girl, unless there was something wrong with her – like Peggy Moss, for instance. She had a squint, poor girl, and the boys used to make fun of her, but Fred used to take her out walking, talked to her for hours. Just to make her feel wanted, I think.

'He was a good man. That's why he never married, I suppose. He was too good for most women, too kind. Most women like to be pushed about a bit – not that your grandad ever pushed me about, but you know what I mean.

'He cried when your father went. I remember him in the kitchen there with your mother, and your mother never spilt a tear until Fred walked up to her and put his arms round her, and then the two of them cried like babies.

'He was always fond of your mother. Perhaps that's why he took to you so much.'

The quiet voice went on as they worked, setting things in order, laying out the memories and rubbing them bright and setting them back in their places: the places that, like the ornaments in the big cold parlour, they would keep for ever now. She's talking him out, Sally thought to herself. She'll talk and talk about him and by the time he's laid in his grave she'll have talked him right away, and he'll belong to the past for ever. That's why she never mourns the others – only Arthur, because she never saw him, she didn't lay him out and talk him into his frame on the wall. He died in circumstances she knew nothing about, and so she can't let him rest in her mind.

The task was done, and he lay there as clean and neat as a man could be. However dirty we are in life, Sally thought, we begin it and end it with a washing. She had not yet begun to assimilate his death; his corpse was as far from being him as any stranger's body she had ever handled, and it was impossible to associate it with a living, thinking, speaking person, with habits and traits and personality. She looked down at him, and could think of nothing to say.

'Well, that seems to finish it,' she said at last. 'The episode is over.' Perhaps that was rather tactless, she misgave, but Gran was far away with her thoughts. 'It seems a strange kind of bargain,' Sally went on, 'four Swedish sailors saved, three Cornish sailors dead. Four saved at the cost of three.'

'That's the way of it,' Gran said. 'You can't choose whether to let your man go out or not, any more than you can choose whether he'll come back. When the sea wants you, he'll take you.'

There was one more laying-out to be done, and Sally did it alone. When she went up to bed that night, she saw what had somehow missed her notice the night before, that her wedding dress was still hanging outside the wardrobe. She took it down from its hanger and held it in her arms for a moment, feeling the smooth material and the crispness of the underskirt, and then she laid it down on the bed and went out. A moment later she returned with an old suitcase whose use had been superseded by a newer, smarter case, and into this, with tissue paper, she carefully folded the white dress. She laid the little flowery hat on top, closed the case, and knelt on the floor to push it under the bed.

As she did something else caught her eye – the photograph in its frame, still lying face down on the floor. She picked it up, and sat back on her heels to look at it. It was a photograph of Jim, enlarged from a snapshot she had taken of him the year before last when they had been walking on the cliffs. He was wearing a cable-sweater, and held a jacket slung over one shoulder. His eyes were screwed up against the sun, and his hair had been blown every which-way by the bright Cornish breeze that blew 364 days of the year over the cliffs. It was a picture full of easy, happy, young life, a bright and windy picture, like the day, like the man himself.

Sally gazed at it for a long time, as if it would give her some answer, and then she opened the case again, put the picture in on top of the dress, closed the case, and pushed it out of sight under the bed.

She stood up, brushed her hands over her knees, and said aloud, 'And that really is the end.'

But there was the slightest note of hesitancy in her voice, as if she were not sure that it mightn't be a question rather than a statement.

CHAPTER FIVE

As often happens when summer lingers on past its time, when the season did change it went straight into winter, and autumn never got a look-in. In a matter of days the cold winds stripped the few deciduous trees of their leaves and the old folk got their winter underwear out of the drawers where they nestled in mothballs. In a matter of days summer and coatlessness was merely a dim memory and Pengarth shrugged off its summer visitors and settled in to the grim season.

Sally felt a kind of relief with the change of season. It seemed easier to bear everything when it wasn't being mocked by blue skies and buttery sunshine; easier to sit snug by the fire with a book than to go for walks along alleys and paths around whose every corner she expected, sickeningly, to meet Jim.

That was the hardest part – simply bringing herself to believe he was dead. 'Dead' didn't seem to mean anything, and she could not shake off the feeling that if she waited long enough, if she revisited all the places they had been to together, he would one day walk in through the door and everything would be as it was. And every day the summer weather, enticement that it was to sociability, had lured her out of doors to the places she and Jim had haunted; to places where the villagers' pity and curiosity could wound her.

With the onset of winter she solved her problem in a kind of a way: she gave up trying to believe it, and simply didn't think about it. She shut her mind off from that part, never alluded to him, never thought about him. As far as it went, it worked. At least it allowed her to get on with her job.

The change of season, while it helped Sally, only made Gran feel restless. It was probably because she had missed her autumn bottling, jamming, and salting which normally tided one over nicely from the summer when all the windows were open and one felt one had everything before one, to the winter when one felt only the onset of age. Gran felt she had been hustled into something, done out of something, and that, coupled with her extra need to be busy in order to bear with the loss of Fred, gave rise to the Great Plan.

Sally, engrossed, perhaps forgivably in the circumstances, with herself, did not notice the symptoms in her grandmother, and the first she knew about the scheme was when Gran presented her with it one evening in late November. Sally was sitting at the table in the kitchen, eating her supper. She had just come in from evening surgery and was tired enough not to notice that Gran seemed excited.

'How was the surgery, Sally?' Gran asked to keep herself from blurting out the news. 'Many in?'

'Not so many really,' Sally said. She had a book propped up against the sauce bottle and was reading it with half an eye, not particularly interested in it, but wanting to finish it because it was due back at the library on Friday. 'The usual sniffles and the annual crop of pregnancies, nothing much else. This dry spell has helped. It's the wet weather that brings them all in – with the sailor's disease,' she added with a grin. She often used the local, unscientific names for diseases which she learnt from Gran because they amused her. Sailor's disease – rheumatism; old man's friend – pneumonia; foggy chest – bronchitis; Doctor Alexander scorned the lay terms and would sooner have to translate as he went along than refer to knee-caps and funny-bones, and he and Sally often had arguments on that score.

'It's having a wet August that does it,' Gran said, referring to the dry spell. 'A wet summer brings a dry winter.'

Sally smiled tolerantly.

'But you always say a dry winter brings on a wet summer. At that rate we'd only ever have the one weather pattern, the same every year.'

'All the same, it's surprising how often it does happen that way,' Gran said. 'Anyway, we'll be thankful for a dry winter this year.' Sally didn't answer, and Gran tried a more direct approach. 'I've been thinking—'

'Um?' Sally said, concentrating on cauliflower cheese.

'I been thinking, this house is really too big for the two of us.'

That caught her attention all right. She looked up, frowning, and said, 'You're not thinking of moving, surely?'

'No, not moving – not moving out, at any rate.'

'What other kind of moving is there?'

'Well, what I had in mind would mean us moving downstairs.'

Sally stared at her, and then shut her book and put it aside. 'All right, out with it. What've you been up to?'

'Well, it first came to me just like that – that the house was too big for two of us. I thought that if we had a wet winter we'd have to move into the front of the house and keep a fire going all the time in here and in the front room. Then I thought, what a pity to let the rest of the house go to seed.'

Without even realizing it, Gran stood up, and began to walk back and forth as she spoke.

'Then it came to me – the house is ideal – the right size, the right position – for a guest house.'

'What!'

'No. Listen before you say anything. It's too big to keep up just for the two of us, what with the price of coal. We'd have to move into part of it, and the damp would get in, and it would be the ruin of the place. But if we opened in the summer as a guest-house, we'd make enough to keep it in decent repair all year round. It's a lovely house, it's attractive from the tourist point of view, and it's right on the harbour front. We'd have no rivals.'

'Well, I can see that – there's only the Anchor after all, and Mrs Treddenick in the High Street – but . . .' Sally mused slowly, and Gran broke in again irrepressibly.

'The way I worked it out was like this: you take my bedroom, and I turn the study into a bedroom for me, and we keep the sitting-room for our sitting-room. Then we knock down the wall between the parlour and the garden-room to make one big room; put a divider across the middle and the front part's the guests' dining-room and the back part's their

45

sitting-room. That keeps their half separate from our half.'

'Not much of a view for their sitting-room,' Sally commented.

'But a lovely view from their dining-room: get them out early in the morning! We could knock a door through the wall here,' she patted it with her hand, 'so we wouldn't have to walk through the passage with their food: straight through, you see!'

'You've been working this out, haven't you,' Sally said, amused at Gran's eagerness.

'For weeks,' Gran admitted. 'Ever since we had those Swedish sailors in and I realized how many we could bed down comfortably.'

'There's no shortage of bedrooms,' Sally agreed, 'and the whole attic for extensions.' She was half joking, but Gran had already been in the attics in her mind's eye.

'That would depend on how business went, but if we needed it we could put another three at least in the attic.'

'What about the pottery – would you turn that into a tea-shop?'

'Mercy, no!' Gran took her seriously, and was shocked. 'The pottery's one of the attractions. All the guests would buy things in the pottery, and take stuff home for their friends. Andy can manage the pottery and we can get him a 'prentice to train up by summer. The pottery would be a big part of the set-up.'

'Well, it sounds possible,' Sally said slowly, thinking it over, and Gran knew by the tone of her voice that she liked the idea. 'But would people come? After all there aren't many visitors to the village in the summer, and they mostly go to people they've stayed with before.'

'Sally, my child, and you a modern miss! Have you never heard of advertising?'

'You mean to advertise?'

'Of course – in all the best magazines. Wealthy people, looking for an unspoilt bit of England, a genuine old pottery would be treasure-trove to them. Peace and quiet, home cooking, fishing, boating – riding up at Overcombe if they want

46

it – we'd have no end to put in the advert. Of course people would come.'

'Home cooking—' Sally grabbed one bit of flotsam from the stream, 'that's you, of course. What about me? Chambermaid?'

'Well, I wasn't sure if you'd want to give up the doctor and come in with me,' Gran began, but Sally grinned and flung out a hand to her.

'Darling Gran, of course I want to come in with you. I think it's very exciting. I'll help you with the cooking, and wait on the guests at meals. And make beds if you like.'

'We'd have to get help, but that wouldn't be difficult. I should think one of the wives wouldn't mind doing the heavy cleaning for a bit of pocket money, and we could get a couple of youngsters to do a bit of part-time chambermaiding during the school holidays. We'd need to do most of it ourselves, of course, or bang goes our profit margin.'

'You're a wonder! Listen to you talking of profit margins as if you'd been in business all your life. It'll be fun, though. When are you thinking of opening? Next summer?'

'Easter!' Gran corrected her sharply.

'Easter?'

'Certainly. Think of all those rich Londoners all wanting to get away for an Easter holiday, and all having to go to Switzerland, just because they don't know about Pengarth.'

'All right,' Sally said, laughing, 'I'll believe you. But, listen, there'll be lots to do. The whole house will need to be redecorated, and then there's this building work you want done, and new beds and mattresses to buy – the plumbing will have to be overhauled – where's all the money coming from? You'll need a hefty dose of capital to get started for Easter.'

'I've been into that,' Gran said, not without a note of smugness, for it pleased her to be able to be a jump ahead of Sally. 'I can get a mortgage on the house itself which will pay for anything we want done, comfortably. Actually,' she added confidingly, her face straightening out of its triumphant grin, 'I had the valuation through today, and it shocked me. I knew

47

property had gone up, but I'd no idea this house was worth that much.'

'What much?' Sally prompted.

'Well, when I went to Mr Soames' – the solicitor – 'to ask if I could get a loan against the house, he asked how much I'd want. I said about three thousand pounds, and he almost laughed, and said, "My dear Mrs Trevose, the house is worth at least twenty thousand". Well, I hardly believed him, but when I saw the valuation – without the pottery, the house alone is worth twenty-four thousand, so they say.'

'Twenty-four!'

'Yes, I thought you'd be surprised. It shows how it pays to take good care of your property. It was well-built to start with, and every Trevose afterwards has kept the place up properly. Not that it needed much, being stone built.'

'Well, you're a rich woman, Gran, and all this time you didn't know it,' Sally said lightly.

'Yes, and you'll be a rich woman when I'm gone,' Gran added. Sally stared, and then rose abruptly to get herself a cup of tea from the pot on the hob. Gran silently cursed herself for being thoughtless, but another part of her mind cursed Sally for being sensitive. She almost mentioned this, but decided against it as Sally came back to the table with the awful blank look on her face that she had been wearing for the past few weeks.

Then, after a short silence in which Gran imagined all sorts of things that might be going through her granddaughter's mind, Sally said, 'A complete change will be good for both of us, you're right in that respect.'

'It did cross my mind, of course,' Gran admitted. 'The house is too quiet when you're out during the day. I need to be busy.'

'Me too,' Sally said. They looked at each other for a moment in the depth of their sympathy, and then, by tacit consent, changed the subject. 'The first thing to do, I think, is to get some estimates on the building and decorating.'

'Building yes, but decorating – no-one's going to stop me

getting my hands on a paintbrush. It's one of things I've always loved doing,' Gran said.

They covered sheets and sheets of paper that evening with drawings and diagrams and sums and trial drafts of the advertisement that was to bring the world to their doorstep – or at least, that part of the world that felt it needed a holiday in the quietest part of Cornwall.

CHAPTER SIX

It was not entirely to be expected that Nicholas – 'Nikko' –
Lee should have elected to spend his holiday in Pengarth
that year, especially as it was one of his boasts that he never
went back to places, and he had been to Pengarth before.

Nikko was a gypsy – actually, a real, full-blooded gypsy,
able to trace back his ancestry, albeit only by hearsay, to a
powerful tribe of wanderers in Turkey a hundred years before. He was pretty impressive on the subject when he wanted
to be, and given the right audience he often fell into a kind
of mimicry of himself that was 'better than going to the
pictures' as one early girlfriend put it.

He was not a tall man, but he had a way of making the
most of his height, and an arrogant way of holding up
his head. His skin was brown, his eyes dark and fringed
with lashes that would not have disgraced a film-star of either
sex. His hair was black and curly; his nose was almost Red-
Indian; his body slim and wiry. Mostly people called him
Nikko because it seemed to suit him, but he had been called
Gyppo, and even on one occasion, Gypsy Nose Lee.

Nikko did not normally take a summer holiday as such, for
he did not do regular work from which he needed a holiday.
His career had been checkered, ranging from builders'
labourer to insurance salesman, but he had for the past two
years been doing what he felt at last to be his real métier –
freelance journalism. This gave him the chance to move
around as he wished, meet people, work his own hours, and –
best of all – write. In the pauses between 'assignments' as he
rather grandly called them, he was working on a novel, a book
which had been his companion since he was sixteen, and had
been re-written so often that the current version bore no
resemblance to the original model. He worked at it in fits and
starts, and a sudden fit, coupled with an early outburst of the
'silly season' when news seemed to be thin on the ground,
made him decide to take the uncharacteristic holiday.

He announced the news one evening to Ted Cooper, junior reporter for the *Wessex Courier*, one of Nikko's more regular sources of income. Like most of the staff of the *Courier*, Cooper was leaning on the bar of the Green Man late one Thursday, having just put the paper to bed, when Nikko strolled in.

'Hello, Nikko. Any news?'

'Not a single new,' Nikko said, propping his elbow on the bar beside the young reporter's. 'Got a copy?'

'Still wet,' said Cooper, passing over a copy of the *Courier*, one of the early copies that were discarded because they didn't print properly until the press got 'warmed up'. 'I haven't checked it yet – you can do it for me.'

'No chance,' Nikko said, turning the pages gingerly – it *was* still wet. 'Do your own work. Besides, the *Courier* wouldn't be the same without your safaris into the backwoods of the O.E.D. How many esses in necessary?'

'Work it out for yourself,' Cooper said quickly.

'That's one of my lines,' Nikko said, then, staring innocently at the ceiling, 'A man could die of thirst in this place.'

'Well, I like that,' Cooper said indignantly. 'You earn twice as much as me, and you've got less to spend it on.'

'Oh, all right, all right,' Nikko said, pretending resignation, and flicked an eyebrow at the barmaid, at which she strolled over, pretending she was coming that way anyway. 'Two light and bitters, and one sapphire glance from your fathomless eyes.'

'You what?' said the barmaid derisively, but she gave a little smirk all the same as she drew the beer.

'Don't you ever give up, Nikko?' Cooper said wearily.

'Well, I was thinking of it,' Nikko said, thumbing over the pages of the *Courier* absently. 'I was thinking, actually, of taking a holiday.'

'Taking what?' Cooper said in astonishment.

'Holiday. Aitch-oh-double-ell – you know how to spell it, being on the *Courier* for so long. Like what people take in the summer, when the works close and the sun shines bright over Mevagissey. Never heard of holidays?'

'Well, yes, I have actually – even been on one – but I can't see what you've got to take a holiday from. A holiday is essentially a change from work, and you obviously don't need that.'

'Har har. Ease off on the funnies and help me choose a bosky dell in which to disport myself for a couple of weeks.'

'Why not turn to page eleven,' Cooper said, absent-mindedly paying for the beer which the barmaid had put down on the counter in front of him. 'There you will find our holiday section in full, techni-black-and-white splendour.'

'I'm already there, treasure, browsing amid the ads,' Nikko said. 'Now, where shall it be? The mud flats of Weston Super Mare? Bracing Torquay? The palmy promenade of Penzance?' He was only half concentrating as he glanced over the page of advertisements for guest houses and holiday camps, but as he turned to the next page, his attention was caught by something, and he exclaimed, 'Hey!'

'What?' Cooper asked, and when Nikko did not answer immediately, he went on, 'Don't say we really have spelt holiday with two ells?'

'No, it's just that this name caught my eye, and I can't think why it sounds familiar.' Cooper looked over his shoulder at where Nikko's forefinger was tapping a rather nicely laid-out advertisement for the Pengarth Pottery – M. Trevose.

'Oh, I know,' Cooper said at once. 'Pengarth was where the lifeboat went out last year, wasn't it? Three men killed to save four or some such thing.'

'Oh yes, of course – Pengarth. And who was Trevose? Anybody?'

'Yes, don't you remember? The grandmother and grand-daughter both bereaved, on the eve of the girl's wedding. We did a big human interest spread on it.'

'Ah, yes, I remember that. That was Sammy Butler's piece. Old slippery Sam oozing adjectives over three columns. Tcha!' He made an indescribable noise of disgust. 'How I loath that expression – "Human Interest". If that's what the humans read, who the hell reads the rest of the paper?'

'Yes, yes of course,' Cooper said quickly, sensing the approach of a hobby horse, and anxious to stop Nikko mounting it. 'But weren't you there yourself? I rather had it in the back of my mind that you did the report on that.'

'No, though I was there, in a manner of speaking. If you remember, I went out in the helicopter to the scene of the rescue. In fact, I never even got to the village. The weather was so rough that we could only take a few long shots, and then we had to put back in to Penzance. I couldn't have got back in time to do a report from the village, so they sent Jim Baker in.'

'We never used the photos, did we?' Cooper asked, frowning in the effort to remember.

'No, they weren't really clear enough. And Jim got a nice snap of some of the lifeboat crew, so they bunged that in instead.' Nikko's eyes went vague for a moment as he remembered that nightmare trip in the helicopter, and imagined what it had been like for the crew out in the same weather in a little cockleshell boat, and gave a slight shiver. 'So,' he said, turning his attention back to the newspaper advertisement, 'that's Trevose. I must say I don't remember it being a hotel.'

'I don't think it was, now you come to mention. Wasn't there a nurse or something?'

'You know what,' Nikko said, coming to a decision, 'I'm sure it wasn't a hotel. And I reckon this is where I'm going to spend my holiday. The brave widows, battling against misfortune, staring a new venture without their menfolk – if there isn't a human interest story to be squeezed out of that, I'll resign and give my camera to slippery Sam for a birthday present.'

'But I thought you hated human interest stories?' Cooper protested.

'So I do. But I want a holiday, and how else am I going to be able to pay for it?'

'Why, you hypocritical so-and-so,' Cooper exclaimed, half in disgust and half in admiration. He envied Nikko his vagabond life, and though he loved working for the paper, he sometimes felt that living with his parents in the house where he was born and writing up weddings and jumble sales lacked something, some vital ingredient of excitement that Nikko somehow managed to grab hold of. 'Well, I hope you enjoy it. Taking photos of the widow in a bikini on their private beach. I can see it all now.'

'So can I,' Nikko said, drained off his pint in one go, thrust the newspaper into his pocket, clapped Cooper on the shoulder, and hurried out.

'Only she wasn't a widow!' Cooper called after him, but the bar door swung closed behind the fast-moving figure before he finished the sentence. 'Man of action!' Cooper snorted derisively.

It was a week later that Nikko finally arrived in Pengarth, alighting at the top of the town from the bus, and carrying in one hand his favourite camera, and in the other a brand-new suitcase. This, in fact, had been a last-minute purchase, for which he had stopped off in Penzance. On his circuitous journey to the little fishing town he had suddenly realized that if the Pottery was a high-class place they probably wouldn't take him in without luggage. So he bought a suitcase, some socks and underpants and a couple of shirts in Marks and Sparks, put the clothes in the suitcase and added the contents of the plastic carrier bag, which was all he had brought with him from his previous lodgings, stopped off again in Woolies for a pair of swimming trunks and a towel, and then went to the bus station.

The bus did not actually go into Pengarth, for the roads were too narrow and too steep, and any big vehicle that tried the descent would either get stuck, or be unable to turn to come back up again. The bus stopped, therefore, in the road that went past the biological research lab, before swinging inland to the nearest railway station, nine miles away.

When Nikko got off the bus he was in company with a group of young people whom he assumed to be holiday-makers, so when they set off down the road he assumed they were heading for the guest-house sector and fell in behind them. They went, however, only a few hundred yards down the road to the gates of the research lab where they paused to produce their passes, and Nikko stopped short, realizing his mistake.

The gate-keeper looked friendly, so Nikko strolled over to

him and asked, 'Can you tell me where the Pengarth Pottery is?'

'Sorry mate, 'aven't a clue,' said the man with a friendly grin. 'Always the way, ennit? 'F you ask the way, the bloke you ask's bound to be a stranger.'

'Right enough,' Nikko said. 'I thought this place was a holiday camp, till I saw them get their passes out. What is it? Atomic station?'

'Not likely. Biological Research. How to live on seaweed. You'll be wanting the village though, won't you?' The gate-keeper became adroitly evasive, and Nikko, not wanting to embarrass him, nodded. 'Well, the village proper is down there, the other way to what you was going, but if you go by the road it winds about for miles. Favourite is to go down the Monks Steps. See that next turning, where that white house is?'

'Yes.'

'Well, you go down there, and about fifty yards down on the right you come to a gap in the wall, and there's one of them "public footpath" signposts – you know what I mean?' Nikko nodded. 'Well, that's the Monks Steps. Lead all the way down, right down to the 'arbour, but if you want the 'Igh Street, it's about the second or third turning off the Steps.'

'Well, thanks very much. That's a great help. I suppose the Steps are very old, lots of legends, eh?'

'I dunno. All I know is that's where the young people do their courting, nights. Them and the cats.'

Nikko laughed. 'Be seeing you.' He lifted a hand in fare-well and walked off swinging his case, and in a few minutes was at the top of the Monks Steps. Since he didn't know where he was going, he decided to take them right to the bottom just to see where they led him, and of course they led him right to the entrance of the Pottery. 'That's a piece of luck,' he said to himself.

Inside the pottery itself, the front part had been turned into a shop by the simple addition of a counter and some shelves against one wall. Here, and on a trestle inside the door, various pieces of pottery were laid out, ranging from beautifully turned vases to chunky stoneware ashtrays, all of them exquisitely painted. Nikko wandered about looking at things, glancing beyond the counter to where a young man in an apron like a butcher's was attending to the furnace, and another man in his twenties was working at the wheel, oblivious to Nikko's presence.

Everyone likes to watch a potter at his wheel, and Nikko, no exception, stood quietly for some time watching the clay rise and stretch as if it had a life of its own. Eventually the lad finished doing whatever he was doing to the furnace, turned and saw Nikko, and hurried over.

'Yessir c'n'yelp you?' he asked all in one breath.

'Well, actually, I was wanting a room for a week or so. I suppose I should have booked in advance, but I only decided to take a break at the last minute.'

'Oh, that's the house you want, next door,' the boy said. The potter allowed his wheel to stop and looked up.

'You'll have to speak to Mrs Trevose. If you go out of the door and round the corner to the right, it's the next door you come to.'

'Thanks very much. Do you happen to know if she's any rooms vacant?'

'I think so. The season proper hasn't started yet, though we've been busier than in past years, after all that in the newspapers.' His blue eyes blazed resentfully for a moment, and Nikko wondered if he somehow knew he was a journalist. But why should the fellow dislike the publicity, if it brought an increase of trade? You'd think he'd be only too glad. . . .

'Well, I'll have to go and see. Thanks very much,' Nikko said, and went out again into the sunshine. He followed directions and found himself in front of the house, and paused to take a look around. It really was an ideal situation for a hotel. The beautiful grey stone house with its gilded slate roof was right on the harbour front, only a broad stretch of cobbles separating it from the bollards and the steep drop to the green water. The bay curved away to the right, to a vista of bobbing masts, sparkling water, and the green-topped cliffs that gave the bay shelter, and above the little town climbed the hill picturesquely. The house itself looked very attractive, with its little mullioned windows, the frames and the open front door painted smartly in black and white, and the window boxes everywhere full of scarlet geraniums and blue lobelia.

A grey tabby cat sat on the whitened front step, blinking in the sunshine, and an enormous herring-gull sat at one end of the roof-tree, staring suspiciously at a couple of choughs who were chasing each other noisily round the chimney at the other end.

'All in all, just what you'd like to expect,' he told himself portentously. He stepped past the cat and into the hall-way, which was dim after the bright sunshine outside, and smelt, predictably, of furniture polish. A reception desk had been set up in the hall, and behind it a board with brass hooks for the keys to the rooms. The floor was of polished wood, and a flight of handsomely shining wooden stairs led to the upper regions from the left of the hall-way. Beyond the desk were several closed doors. On the desk was a register, closed, a bowl of pink roses, and a hand bell of the sort that teachers at his junior school rang at the end of playtime.

Smiling to himself at the recollection, Nikko put down his case, picked up the bell, and rang it, startling himself at the loudness of the noise in the silent house. The cat got up from the doorstep, gave him an affronted look, and walked off round the corner, and at the same time one of the doors opened and a girl came into the hall.

'Hello. What can I do for you?' she asked, smiling pleasantly.

'I was wondering if you have a room spare,' Nikko said. 'For a couple of weeks.'

'I think we can manage that,' said the girl. She came down the hall, crossing a band of sunlight from the stairway window, and went behind the desk to get out the large diary in which the bookings were recorded. Nikko watched her, transfixed, for she was, without a doubt, the most beautiful girl he had ever seen in real life. Having consulted the diary, she raised her speedwell-blue eyes to his. 'Yes, we do have a room vacant. For two weeks, was it you said?' asked Sally.

'Two weeks at least,' said Nikko.

CHAPTER SEVEN

Sally glanced at him, amused. 'At least? You sound very vehement about it. Not on the run, are you?'

'Only from civilization,' the young man said. She almost made a tart remark about Cornish people being as civilized as anyone, if not more so, but managed to restrain herself in time. Usually she found it easy to be polite to the guests, and remember that, while they liked to talk they didn't like to be answered, let alone answered back. To most of the guests, the house staff were a kind of defenceless captive audience, and Sally had learnt to keep her peace. But this young man, over-handsome as he was, with that arrogant lift of the head, and that self-assured tone to his voice that Londoners so often used to people they thought of as 'the natives'; this young man she could feel was going to get under her skin.

'Well, I have a very nice single room vacant at the moment, but that's only vacant for two weeks. If you like, you can have that for now, and then at the end of the fortnight, change into another room, which will be a double. Or you can have the double now, if you like, right through.'

'I'll have the single,' Nikko said. 'I don't mind swapping.'

'Will you want an evening meal, or bed and breakfast only?' Sally asked, pretending not to notice the way he was looking at her. She hoped he would not want evening meal as well, and added, 'There are a couple of very nice restaurants in the town, and you can get pub meals at the Anchor, just down the road.'

'I'll take the evening meal here, thanks. I'm sure it will be excellent.' More chance to talk to her if I'm here in the evenings too, he thought.

'Oh, it will be excellent, all right,' Sally said, resigning herself. 'My grandmother does all the cooking, and she's first class. Will you sign here please.'

She swung the register round to face him, held out a biro with one hand and pointed to the next space with the other.

Nikko wrote his name and address and handed back the pen, and Sally swung the register back again and looked at it.

'Nicholas Lee is the name,' Nikko said, in case she couldn't read the writing. 'Everyone calls me Nikko.'

'I'll show you your room, Mr Lee,' Sally said politely, reaching a key off the board and coming round to his side of the desk. She picked up his case and started up the stairs without a second glance at him. Nikko shrugged and followed.

'Are you the owner, the Miss Trevose in the advertisement?' Nikko asked innocently.

'My grandmother, Mrs Trevose, is the owner of the business, but I help her run it,' Sally said. 'I am Miss Trevose, yes.'

She reached the first floor and turned left, towards the front of the house, and opened the second door.

'This is your room. The bathroom and toilets are next door, and there are toilets also on the second floor and downstairs.'

Nikko followed her in, and could not forbear to exclaim, 'Oh, this is lovely.'

'Yes, it is pretty, isn't it,' Sally said, pleased despite herself. 'I've always liked this room.'

It was small, and perfectly square, and the walls and ceilings were painted white to give the impression of more room. Set in the middle of the front wall was the single mullioned window, which stood open so that the fresh-smelling breeze blew in fluttering the curtains. It looked out over the harbour, and even from where he stood Nikko caught a glimpse of the sparkling sea, the blue sky, and the vivid red geraniums in the window box outside.

The floor was of dark polished wood, that gleamed richly in contrast to the white walls. There was a wardrobe of dark wood too, a small two-drawer chest with a mirror against one wall, on which stood another bowl of roses, yellow this time. The bed was covered with a spread which matched the curtains, both being of a bright peacock blue, wonderfully refreshing against the almost black and white of the room, and there was a small bedside rug on the floor which was white too. The whole effect was uncluttered, restful, and attractive.

'It's lovely,' Nikko repeated, walking further in and looking around.

'The rug's awfully impractical,' Sally said with a small sigh, 'but it just finished the room off so perfectly I couldn't resist it.' She had had a lovely time with Gran, redecorating the rooms and arranging the furniture, and Gran had wanted so much to do the same thing that they had had to share the rooms out between them, with the result that half the bedrooms had the unmistakable Gran touch about them, and the other half were pure Sally, and both the women eagerly collected the guests' comments about the decor and swapped them in a manner of friendly rivalry.

Sally came back to the present with a little shake, and became business-like again, leaving Nikko to wonder what had been going through her mind during the fascinating moment when she had stood staring reflectively at the white rug with a small smile playing about her lips. 'Now, before I leave you to settle down, if you would like to come with me I'll just show you where the dining-room is, and the lounge and the downstairs toilet.'

Leaving his case, Nikko followed her out again, and downstairs, where she opened doors off the hall and revealed to him the functional and well-polished dining-room ('Breakfast is at eight, and dinner at seven, though you can dine earlier by arrangement if you want to go into one of the towns for the cinema or something'), the small lobby with the hand basin and toilet, matching yellow towel and curtains, which had been cleverly installed in the place of the usual cupboard under the stairs, and the lounge, floral patterned chintz, eggshell green distemper, some excellent water-colours on the wall ('They're by a local artist. They're all for sale – the prices are on them') and the inevitable television.

'Well, that covers everything for now, I think,' Sally said, leading him back into the hall and turning to him with a pleasant smile that was three-quarters professional. This kind of thing wasn't entirely new to her. There had been a certain amount of it involved in being a nurse and a medical receptionist.

She was standing in the patch of sunshine from the hall

window, and it lit her red-gold hair to glory. Nikko felt his pulse quicken. 'If there's anything you want,' she went on, 'don't hesitate to ask.'

'Well, there is something,' Nikko said, looking straight into her eyes. He saw her smile freeze ever so slightly, and in a spirit of mischief held her in suspense for a few seconds before he said, 'I'm a photo fanatic, and I would be grateful if you'd let me take a picture of you from outside, standing at the door.'

'Yes, of course,' Sally said, still politely. He had his camera still hanging over his shoulder – he was never without it – and he led the way out of the front door.

'Just stand in the doorway, would you? That's fine.'

He backed off, flipped the lens cap off, and focused. The cat came back round the corner, and Sally scooped it up and held it in her arms, and he wondered if she had ever done any modelling, for she seemed to be a natural for it. She leaned slightly against the door-post, the cat in her arms, looking away from the camera towards the cliffs, completely relaxed and natural. Nikko stooped down, took a shot, and then slipped on the zoom lens and took a close-up of her head and shoulders.

'Thanks a lot,' he said, walking back towards her while putting the lens cap back on. Sally released the cat, who shook himself indignantly and continued on the way she had interrupted, and gave a slightly sarcastic smile.

'Will there be anything else?' she asked. He smiled as disarmingly as he knew how.

'Everything's fine, thanks,' he said.

'Then I must get on,' she said. 'I'll see you at dinner. Seven o'clock.'

'Yes, I remember.'

Sally went in and disappeared into the dark regions beyond the hall, and Nikko went back up to his room and, for want of anything better to do, unpacked and put away his few belongings. I'll have a look round before dinner, he thought. And at dinner I must try and make a better impression on her. She's beautiful – and how! – but I can see her and me having a bust-up before long. I'll end up giving her a smacking, I can see.

Sally meanwhile was in the kitchen, cutting up tomatoes with the savagery she would like to have used in chopping up conceited, arrogant, over-handsome playboys who thought they were god's gift to women, and who thought every woman would come running to them as soon as they lifted a little finger. The first impression each had made on the other was not exactly propitious.

On the day after his arrival Nikko woke early, and for a moment lay pondering over the events of the previous evening – or rather, non-events. He had failed completely to get anywhere near Sally. She had served the guests in the dining-room – dressed very fetchingly in a traditional black dress and white frilly apron – but had been very brisk and formal, and had said no more to him than 'Would you prefer salad or roast lamb?' and 'Black or white?' Seeing that she was serving all the guests single-handed, he hardly liked to delay her with chat, even if he could have got her to stand still long enough to engage her attention.

He banked on lingering over his coffee until the other guests had gone and then talking to her while she cleared away – perhaps, he decided, he would even offer to help her, and that way gain admittance to the staff quarters; but his plan was foiled, for after she had brought in the coffee she did not appear again, and instead a skinny kid of about thirteen came in to clear up – a local child earning pocket money, he supposed. Annoyed, he took his coffee and drifted with the other guests into the lounge to smoke, but the television there annoyed him, and he decided to go out. He hung around the hall for quite a while, but Sally did not pass through, and he could hardly penetrate the private quarters without some kind of encouragement or invitation. By nine he had given up, and he went out and walked along the quayside as far as the Anchor hotel.

He had found that, too, rather disappointing, being full of holidaymakers and the local 'smart set'. The saloon bar had been done out with imitation lobster pots, and fish nets draping the ceiling, and port and starboard lamps flanking the bar, but when he fled to the public bar he found it had been spoilt too, with a juke box and two fruit machines, and it was full of hearty young scientists from the Research Institute, or whatever it was called, and their girlfriends. And then, to cap it all, he had found out about the ten o'clock closing time. There seemed nothing for it but to go to bed; and that early bedtime was principally what led him to wake so early.

He got out of bed and went across to the window and swung the casement open. The sun had not yet risen, but the sky was full of a clear silvery light, overhead already darkening into blue. It was going to be a scorcher. It was so quiet that Nikko could hear the sighing of the waves and the crying of the seagulls way over on the headland; the air was cool and fresh and the sea sparkled calmly right out to the horizon.

A quiet click directly below him made him stiffen, suddenly alert, and leaning cautiously out he looked directly down. His window was over the front door – it was that door being opened that he had heard, and as he looked down he saw Sally step out onto the cobbled quayside and walk away towards the headland. She had a rolled towel under one arm – she must be going swimming.

Nikko could move like lightning when he wanted. It took him only seconds to drag on underpants and jeans, tee-shirt and sandals. He grabbed the trunks and towel he had bought, with such foresight, the day before, and, out of sheer force of habit, his camera, and was down the stairs so quickly that by the time he got outside, Sally was just at the corner of the harbour.

Nikko hurried to get nearer her, keeping in against the buildings in case she should turn, but she did not, and when he had narrowed her lead to a comfortable gap he dropped to her speed and padded along quietly behind her. The shadows law deep and cold under the houses, intensifying as the sun rose, so that the quay was marked out in slices of warm gold and cool black. At the end of the harbour Sally turned down a narrow lane and disappeared from his view, and he ran as far as the corner and was just in time to see her turning off to the left further up the lane.

The next ten minutes were trying for him, because she was making a tacking kind of journey in and out of the little houses and lanes, following a route well known to her but unknown to Nikko. If only he had known where she was heading for he could have made his own way – he had a good sense of direction – but the place was strange to him, and he had to rely on keeping her in sight.

They came out at last where the village ran out onto the lower slope of the green cliff to the west of Pengarth, and just as Nikko was breathing a sigh of relief, Sally stopped ahead of him on the chalk path she was following up the slope, turned and waited for him. Feeling rather foolish he walked towards her, and she stood, arms akimbo, watching him rather grimly. The sun was lighting her hair to a gold dazzle; her limbs were golden brown against the blue shorts and tee-shirt; her feet were bare and brown against the white chalk; Nikko admired her all over again.

He stopped, face to face with her, a foot apart, and they considered each other without speaking. Then he said, 'How did you know I was following you?' It was a good opening, an implied compliment.

'Your sandals squeak,' she replied curtly. 'How did you know I was going out?'

'I didn't actually. I was looking out of the window when you came out, and I decided I'd like a swim too. So I followed you.'

'Then why all the stealth? All this James Bond business?'

'I wasn't sure you'd let me come,' Nikko said, giving her his Disarming Smile. She looked stonily at him, still fully armed. 'So I thought I'd see where you go to swim and then just turn up. I hope you don't mind?' He made it as apologetic as possible; his expression radiated such innocence as to be almost demure. Sally, though she felt exasperated at the invasion of her privacy, was struggling with inner laughter, because he was so transparent.

'I do mind being followed and spied on. Of course I do,' she said. 'But – since you're here, you can come along. But you must behave yourself.'

'Yes mummy,' he said, still more demurely. He felt safe

64

now – he had seen the laugh she was struggling with around the corners of her mouth. He fell in beside her, and they trudged up the chalky track together. Nikko, slipping a little as the jagged stones skidded from under his feet, wondered how she managed with no shoes.

'Anyway, what are you doing up so early?' Sally asked after a moment. 'I get up early for that very reason – to miss the visitors.'

'I went to bed early,' Nikko said. 'Not from choice particularly, but the pub closed at ten, of all ungodly hours, and I can only sleep so long.'

'Yes, they're always strict with visitors. Where were you, the Anchor?'

'Yes.'

'Like it?'

'No.' He was so emphatic that she laughed.

'Well, you must be one of us then. There are much nicer pubs in the town, and the licensing hours are flexible as long as there aren't any furriners about.'

'Where you go?'

'Where I go, when I go. But I don't much. Not any more.'

Ah, Nikko thought, I've come nearer to it now. Her last three words had an echo of sadness in them, the first hint he had had from her of anything in her past in the nature of a shadow.

'Perhaps you'd show me, one evening?' he said gently, tentatively.

'Perhaps,' she said, not encouragingly.

'Perhaps if you would show me some of your pubs one evening, I could reciprocate another evening by taking you out to dinner?'

'I have plenty to do in the evenings,' she said, a little more sharply than was necessary, and that piece of clumsiness – for such it was – revealed a lot to him. She did not want favours done. With sudden insight he imagined how hard it must have been for her to live in this closed community after such a public kind of tragedy. He imagined all the tactless tact, the pity, the people trying to 'take her out of herself', and could not wonder that she rejected his advances.

No, the way round her was to ask her help, not to offer her anything, he thought. He tucked the idea away, ready to be worked on when the right moment came.

They reached the top of the slope, and Nikko found himself on the cliff top, with the sea far below him like a wrinkled silver skin, and the fresh sea wind blowing up into his face. Sally stopped, and they both looked out at the dazzling view for a while.

'Lovely, lovely,' he said. 'I wish I had a filter with me; but that brightness would be too much without one, even if I stopped right down.'

'You really are a keen photographer, aren't you?' Sally said with an amused smile. 'Even when you come out for a swim you can't leave it behind.'

'Where do you swim, anyway?' Nikko asked lightly.

'Down there. It's a bit of a scramble. I hope you don't break your lens. There used to be steps cut, but they've worn away over the years.'

'Don't worry about me, I'll manage,' Nikko said.

'I wasn't worrying,' Sally answered.

Sally led the way down a kind of rabbit-path that kinked backwards and forwards across the cliff, following the approximate line of a rock fault. Here and there Nikko found the remains of rudimentary steps, some of them even reinforced with rusty iron bars, but in other places they had been washed or eroded away, and he had no breath or attention for anything but the descent. Sally had obviously done this hundreds of times, for she was never in doubt as to the next step, even when there was a choice of several tracks, as happened on the less steep parts. She jinked like a hare, sometimes dropping vertically onto a small foothold, sometimes jumping a gap over a dizzy drop. Nikko, nimble as he was, was hard put to it to keep up with her, and was very glad when they reached the safety of the small pebbly beach at the foot of the cliff.

The beach was cool, still in its own shadow, but Sally said, 'The sun will be round the point by the time we're in.'

'I bet the water's cold,' Nikko said.

'It is. Scared?'

66

'Don't be silly. I'll race you – first in.'

'You wouldn't have a chance,' Sally declined. 'I've got my costume on under this – you've got to change.'

'How do you know I've got to change?'

'Because I can see your trunks sticking out of your towel, idiot.'

'You should have been the detective, not me,' Nikko said caustically. He noticed that they seemed to be getting on well – he must try not to strike any wrong notes now.

Sally stripped off her shorts and shirt in one casual movement, and then stood waiting for him, looking politely away as he struggled to get into his trunks without exposing himself too much. After a minute she said, 'You needn't bother with the towel. I shan't look round until you tell me.'

'You'd better not,' he said, thankful to be able to dispense with all that modesty, but willing to bet he could guess what her expression was. 'All right, I'm decent again.'

Sally turned and looked at him appraisingly. 'Yes,' she said at last, 'you're nicely built. You must keep yourself fit.'

'I try to,' he said, thankful that he had shaved before dinner last night, and that his curly hair always looked much the same whether it had been combed or not. 'Mind if I take a picture of you?'

'Let me take one of you,' she said, holding out her hand. It was one of Nikko's idiosyncrasies that he couldn't bear anyone else touching his cameras, and he automatically drew it closer to him.

'I can't spare the film,' he said quickly, and then deciding this was the moment for a little judicious honesty, 'I'm not a photography maniac the way you think – it's my living. I'm a journalist, you see.'

'Oh, I see,' Sally said. She sounded doubtful and he could see from her expression that her quick brain was racing to fit things together. 'That would explain why you always carry it about. But why, in that case, take pictures of me?'

'I take pictures of everything that might make a good picture,' Nikko said, taking the opportunity of getting her into focus while he talked. 'You see, I'm a freelance journalist, and I have to make money where I can, and there's often

67

a market for good pictures even where there's no news attached. On the other hand, you may turn out to be a good story as well. So I can't lose.' The sun came round the point, and Sally was thrown into sharp relief, one half of her reddish gold from the sun and the other half dark in shadow. 'Stay still a moment,' he said. Snap – wind – snap – wind. 'Tell me when I can move,' Sally said tartly.

'Okay I've done now – for the moment. Let's have a swim,' Nikko said. He put the lens cap on, laid the camera down on his clothes, and ran towards the water.

It was freezing, and the shock of getting in deprived him of speech for some minutes. Sally swam round him in circles, laughing mockingly, and when he made a clumsy dart at her she glided away from him, disappeared under water, and surfaced again twenty yards further out. She could swim like a dolphin, he realized; he could only admire her, for he was himself an uninspired swimmer, able to keep going for long periods, but neither fast nor stylish. At length she came back in towards him, and they basked side by side in the sunlit strip at the mouth of the tiny cove.

'What are you down here for?' Sally asked suddenly.

'Why shouldn't I be here?'

'I mean, are you on holiday, or are you working? You're a puzzle to me. This isn't the kind of place I would think you'd like to holiday in, but on the other hand, there isn't anything to report in these parts either.'

'Well, it's a bit of each, actually. I am here mainly for a holiday, but I thought there might be something I could make a story out of. Smugglers, pirates, hidden treasure –' he spoke lightly so that she could think he was joking if she wanted, but she looked at him solemnly – 'it's the silly season, and all the papers are short of copy.' She trod water calmly, listening and giving nothing away. He took a further step onto the thin ice. 'There was a big story here last year – I might be able to get something on those lines – a background story from someone involved perhaps—'

That was as far as he got before the ice cracked. Sally rolled over and swam away from him towards the shore. He floundered after her and followed her up the beach so closely that when she stopped abruptly and turned on him he skidded on the pebbles and fell on one knee. She looked down at him, her eyes like blue ice.

'I'm glad I didn't entirely believe you before. Now I know why you're skulking about after me, and taking photos, and smarming up to me.'

'Now listen, you don't understand—' Nikko began, but Sally cut him short.

'No, you listen. I almost began to like you just now, and I shall find it very difficult to forgive you for that. I know you have your living to make like anyone else, and if you'd come to me honestly I might have helped you. But the way you've gone about things is worse than dishonest – it's in damn bad taste!'

With that Sally snatched up her towel, shirt and shorts, and, wet as she was, started off up the cliff, leaving Nikko on the beach staring after her.

'Damn,' he said to himself. 'That's torn it.' He watched her climb quickly, rubbing herself dry with one hand as she went, and his irritation grew, against himself for being clumsy and against her for being – well, for being what she was. 'Silly bitch,' he said to himself, but there was wistfulness rather than conviction in his tone.

CHAPTER EIGHT

Back at the house Sally washed, rinsed out her bathing things, dressed, and went straight down to the kitchen, to find Gran already there, with the two big kettles on the gas stove almost boiling, laying out the trays for the early morning tea. The routine was that they both mucked in with this task, and then had their own breakfast in the kitchen before starting the guests', though often they found they hadn't time to sit down to their breakfast properly, but ate it on the move while they worked.

'Good swim dear?' Gran said by way of greeting. 'It's going to be hot later – you were wise to go early.'

'Umph!' Sally's attempt at a non-committal reply only revealed to Gran that she was in a bad mood. She looked covertly at her granddaughter as the latter finished laying up the trays, but said nothing. It was usually better to let Sally tell it herself, rather than worm it out of her.

'– three, four, five. That's right isn't it?' Sally counted as she crashed spoons into saucers all round.

'Yes, if the new guest doesn't want tea. Did you remember to ask him last night?'

'I asked him all right,' Sally said, and her anger boiled over as abruptly as a kettle. 'But he won't be wanting it this morning. He'll be lucky to get back in time for breakfast.'

'Why, Sally, whatever's wrong?'

'Kettle's boiling – here, I'll get it,' Sally said, but Gran pushed her back firmly.

'No, no, I'll do it. You'd only scald yourself.' She slid her hand into a cloth, against the steam and, picking up the first of the big black kettles, poured a steady stream of boiling water into each of the little teapots in turn. 'What were you saying about the new guest? Has there been an accident?' she asked meanwhile.

'Not yet, but there will be if he comes near me again,' Sally snorted. Gran raised one eyebrow questioningly, and

70

Sally said, 'Oh, I'll tell you all about it – but let's get these trays up first. I'll do the upstairs ones, if you'll bring them to the first landing.'

They stacked the trays and went together up the quiet stairs to the first floor, and here Gran put hers down and went along to the first-floor guests with their tray, and Sally went on upstairs to do the four rooms on the second floor and attic, while Gran went back down to the kitchen to start breakfast for the two of them. Sally returned a few minutes later and began savagely cutting bread while Gran did their bacon and eggs.

'I should have guessed when he came yesterday that he wasn't the type to come here for a holiday,' she said. 'Andy came in specially to warn me against him—'

'Well, Sally, that's nothing to be wondered at. Andy croons over you like a cat with one kitten.'

'That doesn't stop him being right now and then.'

'All right, but what's this guest done? What's his name – Lee, isn't it?'

'Lee. When I went out for a swim today he followed me. I don't know how he knew I was going, but I wasn't fifty yards from the door when he came out and started creeping along behind me, slinking along by the wall like an old tom cat.'

'And what did you do?'

'I let on I hadn't noticed him, to see what he'd do. He followed me all the way, and when I jumped him he pretended he was just longing for a swim, and when I asked why he didn't call me to wait for him he said he wasn't sure I'd like him tagging along.'

'He was probably right,' Gran said, amused. 'You aren't very nice to young men as a rule.'

'Well, even if he was right, surely that's all the more reason to keep away from me? But anyway, that's not what really infuriated me.'

'Well, what was it then?'

'When we got down to the beach he was being very charming and amusing and smarming up to me with the best of

71

them. And then he let it out that he was a journalist, and started trying to worm a story out of me.'

'Really!' Gran considered. 'That was rather tactless of him. About the storm, you mean?'

'Tactless you call it! What he wanted was a sickening inside story of what it feels like to lose your fiancé on the eve of your wedding.' Sally buttered the bread she had cut with fierce swipes of the knife, and heaped the buttered slices on a plate which she took into the dining-room. Gran heard someone – presumably the new guest – come into the hall from the street, heard a few words exchanged, and then Sally came back into the kitchen with her cheeks pink with anger.

After a short silence, during which Gran slapped their breakfasts onto plates and put them on the table, she said gently, 'Sally, dear, why are you so angry with the boy? He's trying to do his job, and even if he's been rather clumsy about it, that surely isn't any reason for getting so upset? You mustn't quarrel with guests, you know – it's bad for trade.'

She meant the last as a gentle tease, but Sally retorted crossly, 'So I've got to be nice to him, simply because he's a guest? I thought this was a hotel, not a brothel.' There was a short, stinging silence, and then Sally, her natural decency overcoming her mood, said quietly, 'I'm sorry, I didn't mean that.' She took a mouthful of food, chewed it with no more appreciation than if it had been sawdust, and then said in a more subdued tone, 'I don't know why I'm so angry about it. I suppose—' she thought for a bit. 'I suppose what upsets me is that I had begun to like him.'

'Well, there's nothing wrong with that.'

'No? Well, I find it rather insulting to discover that all he wants me for is a rotten story for his rotten paper, and that he isn't the least interested in me for myself.'

'I can see why you think that,' Gran said judiciously, 'but I don't think it's necessarily true. You probably wouldn't even think it if you weren't so prickly. What *is* the matter, Sally? You used to be able to laugh at things.'

Sally pushed her plate away and poured a cup of tea,

watching the golden crescent of liquid that curved from the spout as if it would tell her something.

'I had that dream again last night,' she said at last. 'I went down for a swim to be alone and think things out, and then *he* came along.'

'Which dream Sally? You have so many of them.' Gran pushed her cup across the table and Sally poured for her too.

'You know the one I mean. About Peter Westernra. I dream they're bringing him in, all broken and bloody, and when I wash the blood off his face it isn't him, it's—' Sally stopped with a shudder. Gran looked at her with an expression part sympathy and part anxiety.

'It's who? You can't say his name, can you? Do you know, you've never once mentioned him, in all these months. You've never said his name. Why can't you let it alone, Sally? Talk about him, talk him out of your system, and then let it alone.'

'I can't,' Sally said helplessly.

'But you must. You're young, you've your whole life ahead of you. You can't go on fretting about him, and getting cross with young men whenever they pay you a compliment. Even poor Andy, who's practically family – you nearly bit his head off the other day when he admired your dress.'

That raised a small smile from Sally. She laid her hand on the table and turned it palm up in a gesture of surrender. 'Well, perhaps. Perhaps you're right.'

'You could make an effort,' Gran urged, following up her advantage.

'What? What should I do?' She forced a smile. 'You'd better tell me quick, because it's a quarter to eight.'

'What! It's never so late!' Gran jumped up, agitated. 'My goodness, they'll be down in no time. Put the milk jugs out, Sally, and the cereal, while I start the bacon.' She hadn't forgotten what she had been saying, though, for as Sally got up to fill the milk jugs for the dining-room, she said over her shoulder. 'I'll tell you what you can do for a start.'

'What?'

'You can be polite to that poor young reporter, and maybe even give him a story, if you're right and that is what he

73

wants. After all, it can't be easy earning your living that way.'

'It isn't easy being me, either.' But she only thought it, she didn't say it.

Nikko turned up for breakfast looking very neat, freshly washed and shaved, his hair partially disciplined, and wearing a brand-new shirt. He looked at Sally with an expression of apology, contrition and humility, but he had the sense not to try to engage her in conversation there, in public, and she served him without speaking to him, and contrived also not to meet his eyes, though his spaniel-gaze fixed on her must have been very difficult not to pay attention to.

She was to find, however, that he did not give up as easily as that, and when all the guests had gone and she was engaged in clearing the tables – always a sticky, crumby job after breakfast, and usually involving a complete change of table linen; she never could understand why people made such a mess at breakfast, were they all still asleep? – he came quietly in to talk to her. She didn't see him at first, for she had her back to the door and he stepped softly, and when she turned with an armful of dirty cloths he made her jump, and she exclaimed in annoyance.

'What are you sneaking up on me for? Go away and let me get on with my work, can't you!' Halfway through, she remembered Gran's exhortation not to quarrel with guests, and tried to modify her tone, with the result that what started off as an expression of sheer temper ended up sounding almost wistful.

'Sally – Miss Trevose – damnit, I don't know what to call you!' Nikko looked strangely ill at ease, and it was mainly this that prevented Sally thrusting past him, that gave him the chance to go on. 'Look, I want to apologize. I've been stupid and tactless, and I'm very sorry.'

Sally looked at him steadily, partly wondering how much he was apologizing for, and partly wondering how much of this was an act, sheer professionalism. Perhaps he read something of what was on her mind, for suddenly he blushed – she would hardly have thought he was able! – and said with a mixture of shame and petulance, 'I'm not

74

much on apologies. I don't often do it. I don't really know how. But I want to say I'm sorry.'

It was the petulance that convinced her of his genuineness, but even so convinced she was not going to make all easy for him.

'Sorry for what?' she asked stonily.

'For upsetting you,' he said. She shook her head.

'Not good enough. That's like saying you're sorry you spilt the bottle of whisky you were looking forward to drinking.'

'What does that mean?' he said coldly. It looked as though there was a new storm building up.

'I should have thought it was obvious. Sorry you upset me merely means you're thinking about yourself again, sorry you queered your pitch. You'll have to try harder than that.'

'You're deliberately misunderstanding me,' he said, as calmly as he could, trying to muster dignity and keep bitten back the sharp words he wanted to loose on her.

'All right, then you must be more precise. What are you sorry for?'

'Look, I'm trying to be sorry. You want to make it hard for me – go ahead, I can't stop you. But I've got a conscience, and whether you believe me or not, I want to apologize for being an oaf back there.'

He gestured with his head to the outside world, and Sally, feeling that she was not in the ideal situation to be dignified, standing there with an armful of sticky tablecloths, allowed a softening of feature to be discernible.

'I see,' she said in a gentler, encouraging sort of tone. How far would he go?

'I came here for a holiday, you see,' Nikko said, settling himself to tell his story, feeling at ease now, feeling his audience was with him rather than against him; practised actor and raconteur that he was, he had a feeling for audience moods. 'I was feeling brassed off with everything, and I wanted a break. But you see, I'm a freelance reporter, and my work is everywhere and always with me.' He had used that phrase before and had found it telling at the right place. He glanced into Sally's face and saw it polite but veiled. He felt obscurely uneasy. Wasn't it going to work, then?

'So you see, I had to have it in mind that there might be a story down here. It could have been anyone in the village, anyone at all – not just you. I wasn't really thinking of getting a story out of you, to tell you the truth – it was rather heavily written at the time, written out really.' This was his honest, man-to-man voice, plain-speaking, couldn't-be-doubted voice; but Sally's experience was that if anyone said 'to tell you the truth' you could be pretty sure that was what they weren't doing. However, she maintained her polite mask and let him carry on hanging himself.

'When I followed you, it was really, truly, because I wanted a swim, and wanted to get to know you better. That's all. I know I should have gone about it differently, and that's why I'm apologizing.' He stopped, and gave her his most endearing smile, but felt all the same that his performance had lacked some vital ingredient. He waited for the applause, the proper reaction; he looked at Sally, and she was looking steadily at him, as if she were studying him, working something out. By god, she was a stunner, he thought, not entirely irrelevantly; the plain clothes she wore – black skirt and plain white blouse – only served to emphasize her brilliant colouring.

'I'm glad you've come out into the open about it,' she said at last, and added with an irony he didn't notice, 'I'm glad you've been honest about it.'

'I'd like to start again on an entirely new footing,' Nikko said quickly, his confidence coming back to him now she seemed to have forgiven him. 'And to mark it, I'd be honoured if you'd let me take you out to dinner somewhere.'

Sally hadn't expected that, and it caught her so off balance that she had blurted out before she could stop herself, 'Oh but I eat here.'

Nikko smiled with a kind of worldly amusement which made her want to hit him, and said, 'But you don't have to, surely? I mean, your grandmother would allow you to eat out one evening, wouldn't she?'

'You know I don't mean that. I have to get the dinner for the guests, that's why I eat here.'

'Every night?'

'Every night.'

It was Nikko's turn to be surprised.

'Don't you ever have an evening off?' he asked, and the difference in his tone now he was asking a genuine question and not playing a part was so marked to Sally that she wondered how he could think he was fooling anyone with his playacting.

'There's never been any reason to,' she said more gently. Of course, the truth was that, like Gran, she tried not to have spare time, but whereas it was natural in a woman of Gran's age, it was an effort and a rebellion in one of Sally's.

'Well, look,' he said, musing, 'the guests' dinner is at seven, isn't it? So you could be all through by eight, couldn't you?'

'There's the clearing up—' she began, but he broke in, 'I'd give a hand with that. If we were ready by eight, we could dine at nine. That's quite a reasonable time for eating out – lots of people dine at nine or even later.' He sounded now genuinely anxious for her to come, and it was that, more than anything, that decided her. She might have agreed to go out of curiosity, or to get her own back in some degree by eating the most expensive meal she could, but in the end she went because – stupid, crazy reason! – because she felt sorry for him. 'What do you say?'

'Well,' she said, feigning reluctance still, 'I'd have to ask Gran – I couldn't leave her on her own without consulting her first,' she hastened to add. 'But if she doesn't mind – yes, all right. I'll come.'

'Marvellous. Great,' he said. He looked genuinely pleased for a moment, and then his face took on its usual expression of sophisticated superior knowledge. 'Where is there to eat? Anywhere decent? I'd better book a table, hadn't I.'

'Leave it for now,' Sally said, growing brisk with the return of her usual manner. 'I'll have to ask Gran before you make any definite plans – and I must get on with my work, or I'll still be making beds at nine o'clock tonight. I'll leave a note for you in your bedroom some time before lunch.'

'Better still, I'll drop by the house at lunchtime, and you

can speak to me in person,' he grinned. 'I'll ring the reception bell.'

'Okay,' Sally said. 'Now, be a good guest and push off, so I can get on.'

'See you later,' he said cheerfully, and walked out, whistling, into the sunshine. Sally gave a great sigh of visualizing complications, and humped the cloths out to the linen basket. Then she gathered her tray full of dirty crockery and carried it into the kitchen.

'What a time you've been,' Gran said, looking up. 'Carrie's nearly finished the washing up, haven't you, Carrie?'

'Yes'n.' Carrie was the smallest, thinnest, shyest fourteen-year-old in the village, but a prodigious worker, who regarded Mrs Trevose as only a step – and a small step at that – below the Queen. She came in during school holidays to give a hand, which served the double purpose, from her mother's point of view of keeping her out of the way, and bringing in a little money to the family exchequer, strained, as always, to strangling point by the steady appearance of new mouths to feed.

'Sorry, Carrie, I got talking. There's not much here actually – just a couple of plates.'

'Yes, miss,' Clarrie said, almost overcome by being apologized to, and added, daringly, 'S'orroight, oi ent finished nearly.'

Sally smiled and slid the plates into the water past Carrie's cloth, and proceeded to the larder where she unloaded the marmalade jars one by one from the tray onto the lower shelf.

'What were you talking about? Was it that young man?' Gran asked.

Sally took a damp cloth to wipe the tray and said, 'Yes, he crept up on me again. Really, he has an instinct for stealth that will end him up in the 'Moor.'

'What did he want, then?'

'To apologize.'

'There!' Gran looked up with a mixture of surprise and gratification at having been right.

'And to ask me out to dinner.'

'Well, that sounds very handsome to me,' Gran said with

78

approval. 'That was the way young men used to do things in the old days, but I'm afraid they don't often have the know-how nowadays. Everything's so slapdash and makeshift.'

Sally grinned.

'Parents used to say the same of their children in the thirties.'

'And they were quite right, I'm sure,' Gran said, smiling herself. 'So he wants to take you out to dinner. What did you say?'

'I said I had to ask you,' Sally said wickedly, making it sound quite other than it was.

'Sally, really! I'm sure he's much too well-aware of people's characters to have believed that one.'

'I've finished now'n,' Carrie said at that point, and Gran startled, having forgotten she was there.

'Oh, yes – good! What a worker you are, Carrie. Would you just do the butter dishes, and then we'll make a start on the bedrooms together.'

'Yes'n.'

'Now Sally,' Gran went on, more quietly, 'what's all this nonsense about asking me?'

'No, really, I said I couldn't just go off like that without consulting you. I said I'd let him know later this morning.'

'Well, naturally I don't mind, if you want to go. When is it, tonight?'

'Yes. He said he'd help clear away after the guests' dinner, and we could leave about eight, and eat about nine.'

'No need to go to those lengths. I can manage very well for one evening, and I'm sure Carrie wouldn't mind dropping over to give me a hand, would you, dear?'

'Oh, no'n. I'd love to, ever so,' Carrie said, and her face gleamed with genuine pleasure. Nights at home were never a pleasure for her, especially Friday nights, when Dad was likely to have been drinking at lunchtime.

'The thing is, do you want to go?' Gran persisted. Sally frowned.

'I think I do. The trouble is, I don't know why.'

Gran threw her hands up in exasperation.

'What a girl! That's what comes of all that psychology you

read at nursing school. Of course you know why, child – because you'll enjoy it! It will be a pleasant evening out.'

Sally laughed.

'I suppose it does sound rather silly, but—'

'No but about it. It sounds extremely silly. You go and have dinner with that young man, and I'll be very surprised if he doesn't turn out to be good company for an evening. Let him take you somewhere special – why not go in to Hamley and eat at that new place – what's it called? – the one with all the rhododendrons—'

'Wheeler's?'

'That's the one. I've heard it's very good.'

'But you'd need a car to get there,' Sally objected.

'Well, get a car then,' Gran said impatiently. 'Ernie Watt will have a car he can lend you. Or let the young man hire a taxi. Don't be mean about these things, Sally. It never pays to be mean on an evening out.'

At this Sally burst into laughter.

'Gran, you're marvellous. You're a born aristocrat! As long as he's paying, why be mean with the money?'

'And I'm right, too. He'll think more of you if you cost him a packet the first night out.'

'First? What do you mean, first? It isn't as though there'll be another,' Sally said sharply, suddenly unreasonably irritated. Gran raised an eyebrow and turned her attention to the table she was in the process of wiping down.

'Well, well, just as you say,' she said peaceably. 'Anyway, you're going to go *this once*?' She emphasized the words ironically. Sally felt defensive, though she didn't know why she should be.

'Yes, I'll go this once.'

'And you'll go to Wheeler's?'

'If I can get him to agree,' she said. Gran gave a smile of what looked at first glance to be relief.

'I'm so glad – I've always wanted to go there, and at least you'll be able to do the honours for the family.'

'So that's what's behind your sudden concern!'

And Sally laughed again. It was extraordinarily nice to be able to laugh again.

CHAPTER NINE

Whatever Nikko's faults – and many people thought them legion – meanness was not one of them.

When Sally said she would come to dinner with him, and would moreover take the evening off to do it properly, he was delighted; and when she expressed a tentative desire to be taken to Wheeler's he agreed immediately. She explained the difficulty in getting to the place, and he equally promptly said that he would hire a car for the evening, that he would arrange everything, that she was not to worry.

'What time would you like to eat? I'll book a table for whatever time you like,' he asked. He seemed bubbling over with eagerness, and Sally found that somehow touching.

'You may not have a choice – it's a very new and very popular place, and it is Friday, after all. Better see how booked up they are before you go promising me anything.'

'All right, but if we have a choice, what time would you like to eat?'

'Oh, about eight, I suppose,' Sally said vaguely. Actually, she had never eaten in the kind of sophisticated places she imagined Nikko haunting in the large cities, and she wasn't sure what was the correct, sophisticated time to choose. Eight seemed to be at least unexceptionable, and they left it at that. He would let her know, as soon as he had telephoned, what time to be ready for the car. Half an hour later, in fact, he rang the bell for her and when she appeared from the nether regions of the house, told her that he had managed to secure a table for eight-thirty, and had ordered the car for seven-thirty, so they could drive out and have a drink somewhere before dinner.

'That's fine,' Sally said, vaguely again, because she had suddenly realized she hadn't a clue what to wear. 'I'll be here on the dot of seven-thirty.'

'I'm looking forward to it.' Nikko's smile seemed a little strained, as if he was trying to keep up something slightly too much for him, and they were both secretly glad of the excuse not to see each other again until then.

Sally's panic over what to wear descended on her at half past six, and lasted for five minutes before she reasoned herself out of it. It rather reminded her of the first grown-up 'date' she had ever had, when she was sixteen. Being then still at school, she had hardly any clothes besides her school uniform, in which she spent most of her time; now, she had hardly anything besides her 'uniform' of working clothes, the black skirts and white blouses, and the black-parlourmaid dress. In fact, as she well knew, she looked very good in black, but since he had seen her serving in a black dress she felt he might with some justice feel insulted if she turned up to dinner in it. It was at that point that the panic set in, and she thought she should have gone out and bought something while the shops were open.

She was lying in her bath at the time – not the ideal time to bathe, since the guests were mostly in, getting ready for their own dinner – and after a moment the luxury of hot water made her relax again. After all, she thought, he won't be in a dinner jacket, because he hasn't got one with him. In fact, she thought, I don't think he's got a suit at all. It isn't for him you need to dress up. And if you were thinking of dressing up for Wheeler's – I'm ashamed of you. Something neat, plain and pretty will do very well, no-one could object to that.

It'll have to do, she answered herself wryly. It's all there is. She heard doors opening and shutting down the corridor, and reluctantly heaved herself up and began soaping quickly. Her hands she scrubbed hard several times to get the in-grained dirt out – they were showing the neglect they had suffered over the past weeks. There's nothing like peeling potatoes for ruining the hands.

Back in her own room, she dusted herself with scented talc, and creamed her face and hands, put on fresh underwear, and then opened her wardrobe door for the inspection. Not much to inspect, she snorted derisively, and after only a moment's hesitation she chose the navy-blue. It was in artificial crêpe, sleeveless, with a cross-over front that dipped sharply enough at the front to make it more of an evening dress, than a day dress. It was knee-length, and just formal enough to make it necessary to wear stockings. She put it on, put on a pair of pale tights and slipped her feet into her plain black-patent shoes, and then went to look at herself in the mirror again.

Yes, the dark colour suited her, showed off her colouring, and the hint of blue in the navy set off her eyes without competing with them – she had to be very careful about anything blue. In fact, she thought crossly, with the added problem of red hair, there was virtually no colour she was safe with, except black and white, which weren't colours anyway, so they were told at school. She sat down at the dressing-table, still staring at herself, and then on an impulse dug in a drawer and pulled out the padded plastic bag in which she kept her make-up, all unused now since she was about nineteen. She pulled out bits and pieces and examined them, several times brought one up to within an inch of her face, and then put it down again. Finally she swept the whole lot back into the bag, and dropped the bag, contents and all, into the waste-paper bin beside her.

What was the matter with her, she thought angrily as she took up her brush and swept it fiercely through her hair. She hadn't worn make-up since she was a silly young thing. Hers was the kind of beauty that was only dulled by cosmetics, and she had known that even at nineteen, but had wanted to keep up with fashion at all cost. She hadn't worried so much about her appearance for years, she hadn't taken so much trouble over an evening out, not even when she was going out with—

Even in her private thoughts she never spoke his name, only thought the vague shape of him. She hadn't taken this kind of trouble over going out with him, but then she had always known him, and didn't have to make an impression. That was it. That had to be it. She couldn't let herself even consider that she might be more than casually interested in this Nicholas Lee person, that it was not because he was a stranger that she was excited at the thought of going out with him.

Her hair gleamed red-gold in the casual curls that suited her, and there was nothing more to be done. She was ready, but it was too early yet. No, wait, after all it was a special occasion – she was visiting Wheeler's for Gran. She gave a little smile, and opened her 'jewel case', a large cigar box with a painted lid that her father had given her to keep her little treasures in when she was only a little girl. Once it had held her prized one-and-sixpenny bus ticket, a lucky stone with a hole in it, a piece of horsehair from the tail of her favourite pony at the riding school; now it was dignified by the title of 'jewel case' though it still held little that was of material value. Out of it she took and put on her gold charm bracelet, which as yet held only six charms because she was fussy about them and only wanted charms that had something to do with the sea, and the plain gold choker necklace that had belonged to her mother.

Yes, that was better. That made it special. Gold suited her, made her look richer, in every sense of the word. Calm now, she took a book to the window and read in the evening light until it was time to go down.

Nikko was already outside, standing with his back to the door and staring reflectively at the car, a red Escort, very shiny and clean, by which alone you could have known it was a hired car, since all the cars belonging to people in Pengarth were covered in winter with wet mud and in summer with dry. Nikko turned as she came out and smiled.

'You look very elegant,' he said, choosing whether by luck or judgement just the right word to allay Sally's fears. 'I'm sorry I can't dress up to you, but I don't have a suit with me. I hope you won't feel ashamed to be seen with me.'

Fishing for compliments? Sally wondered to herself, and then dismissed the thought. Mustn't be mean with the fellow.

'Of course not,' she said. 'You look very well yourself.' If she had but known it, Nikko's clothes had caused him far more anguish than hers did her, and in fact almost everything he had on was new, bought that day. He was wearing grey herringbone-tweed trousers, a white shirt and a dark-blue tie, and a v-necked sweater in a lovely shade of cobalt blue. He looked very well, as Sally had said, and she concentrated on the car to take her mind off that.

'They've done you proud with the car, haven't they,' Sally said, and as she walked forward Nikko sprang before her and opened the door. The inside was immaculate too, which again was different from any other car she had ever been in – they had all been full of cigarette-ends and old newspapers, gum-boots and rags, oily overalls and buckets of fish-meal, toy trains and tattered Beanos.

'What were you smiling at?' Nikko asked as he slid into the driving seat beside her.

'I was just thinking of the usual state of the inside of people's cars round these parts. They'd practically need decontaminating before you could get in in decent clothes.'

'I know the sort of thing you mean,' Nikko said as he started up and drove along the quay. 'The only trouble is, the sort of people who clean their cars to a state like this one are usually the kind who can't talk about anything else. I don't know what's worse – getting covered in jam and dog-hairs, or having to listen to a blow-by-blow account of the latest gear-box trouble.'

Sally laughed. 'I know what you mean.'

'That's one of the reasons I never got a car,' Nikko said modestly.

Sez you, Sally retorted vulgarly, but only inside her head.

'What should I call you, by the way?' Nikko asked, changing down to second for the steep climb up the town.

'Call me Sally, of course. I can't insist on formality if you're taking me out to dinner – especially since it's the most expensive restaurant in Cornwall we're going to.' She waited until he had swung safely out onto the main road into the thin stream of traffic there, and then said, 'And what should I call you, Mr Nicholas Lee?'

'My friends call me Nikko,' he said, 'which is convenient if not flattering. I don't mind what you call me.'

'Okay,' she said, 'I'll think of something.'

They arrived at Wheeler's just on eight o'clock and pulled up in the gravelled yard under the high banks of rhododendrons for which the area was famous. Wheeler's was a single-

85

storey building, rather in the style of a Swiss chalet, set into a semi-circular, twelve-feet-high hedge of crimson rhododendrons, and out at the back the lawn was edged with more bushes of them in every colour imaginable. The blooms were as big as soup plates, and vivid as flames in the evening light.

'Beautiful, isn't it?' Sally said as she stood waiting for Nikko to lock the car door. He straightened up and looked around, and then at Sally. His eyes lit and he said 'Yes' softly, leaving her in doubt as to whether he meant what she meant.

'There are more out the back. We can have a drink on the lawn until our table's ready, if you like.'

'You seem to know a lot about the place – I thought you'd never been here?' Nikko asked.

'There was a write-up on the place, when it first opened, in *Country Life*. Gran always reads that, cover to cover, and she showed this particular article to me. It was the first restaurant of this type ever to be opened in these parts.'

'What do you mean, "of this type"?' Nikko asked as they walked over the scrunching gravel towards the entrance.

'Well, I mean, all the other eating places hereabouts are either fish restaurants, or just working-men's cafés. Nothing smart or luxurious.'

'A bold venture, then? I hope they succeed in it. A bit risky, I would have thought.'

'Yes, we thought that too, especially since it isn't even on a main road. But it's done well since they opened – we must just see how they get on when the novelty's worn off. People come from great distances to eat here, anyway.'

They were shown by a waiter through the hall to the back lawn where they sat at a table facing out towards the famous rhododendrons. Fairy lights were run discreetly round from tree to tree, not lit yet since dusk hadn't fallen; the lawn was venerable, but with a few daisies here and there, so perfectly placed that they might have been planted deliberately; and round the edge of it was a low border of alysum, lobelia, french marigolds, and pansies, to counterbalance the height and darkness of the hedges.

The waiter brought them their drinks – sherry for Sally,

a martini for Nikko – and they sipped them in silence as they looked round at the lovely scene. Then Nikko picked up the conversation where it had left off.

'So who comes here, then? The holiday-makers?'

'Yes, a lot of those do. The place is well advertised, of course. But there are lots of people who own houses in this part of the country – some have retired here, some commute to towns to work, some have a place in London, even, and use it as a weekend house – and they are all pretty well-off. Before Wheeler's, they hadn't anywhere to go if they wanted to eat out, unless they drove quite a distance into one of the towns.'

'So instead of that, they come here.'

'Yes. And, according to the article, they've done a lot of weddings here, too. I should think it must be a nice place to have your reception. Imagine the wedding pictures on the lawn here, with all that colour in the background.'

They looked again in silence at the view, and Nikko felt for the first time some kind of sympathy for her, for what had happened to her last year. He glanced secretly at her face – she really was stunningly beautiful! – and wondered if she was thinking about that too. He planned a roundabout route of attack, making use, like a good soldier, of the conversational features of the ground they had covered to conceal his movements.

'I suppose your grandmother must take a lot of interest in this kind of thing, being a hotelier herself?'

'Well, she does, I suppose, but she always read *Country Life*, ever since she was first married. She used to be in service, you see, as a girl, and it reminded her of the way the people she served used to live, to read about parties and balls and shooting and hunting and all that kind of thing.' Sally stretched out her legs comfortably in front of her, crossing her neat ankles, feeling quite relaxed now. 'She always had a soft spot for it – that's why she advertised in it when we opened. Where did you see the advert, by the way?'

'In the *Wessex Courier*, actually.'

'Is that one of the papers you work for?' Sally asked.

Nikko, however, was not going to be diverted on to himself just yet.

'Yes, it is, actually. I picked the ad out from the holiday page, mainly because I didn't remember having seen it before.'

'No reason why you should, was there?'

Nikko smiled, wondering if she had divined his purpose. 'No, but I read that paper so often that I know all the names in it back to front. Why didn't your grandmother advertise in it before? It's got one of the biggest circulations in Wessex.'

'She started off advertising in the magazines and the London weeklies. We thought we'd do better from that kind of trade than local people, expecially for the Easter break. We only opened at Easter, you know.'

'Really? – ah, that explains it then!'

'Explains what?'

'Why I had this idea you were a nurse. I had it in the back of my mind that I'd read you were a nurse, and I couldn't understand it, when I found you and your grandmother running this hotel, and doing it as if you'd been in the trade all your lives.'

Sally, who had been about to be cross at Nikko's reading about her in the papers, was deflected – as he knew she would be – by the compliment on their efficiency in the boarding-house business.

'Actually, it isn't difficult, only hard work. The costing is just common sense, and for the rest, you only have to think what you'd like if you went to stay in a boarding house, and there you are.'

'But what made your grandmother suddenly go in for it? Was it lack of funds – income, I mean?'

'Well, yes, partly. But mainly it was that, with Uncle Fred gone, Gran found the house too big and lonely for her. She thought she'd have to shut up part of it and live in a couple of rooms only, and she said if she did that the rest of the house would begin to decay.'

Nikko nodded. 'That usually happens – far quicker than you'd expect.'

'Yes. She couldn't bear to think of the house falling into disrepair, after it'd been kept so well for generations – it's been the Trevose family house for hundreds of years, you know. So she hit on this plan.'

'I think that's marvellous, to come fighting back after such a blow,' Nikko said warmly, knowing that Sally had great admiration for her grandmother.

'Gran's like that,' Sally said, her eyes smiling. 'She's terribly brave; it's almost frightening sometimes.'

'She was wise to give herself something to do like that, so that she didn't brood. But tell me, you were a nurse before, weren't you? What made you give that up and go in with Gran?'

'I could hardly not go in, could I? She couldn't run it single-handed, and if she'd had to employ someone, that would reduce the profits very steeply. Besides, I liked the idea. I wanted a change, and this seemed like a heaven-sent opportunity.'

At that moment the waiter came out to them to tell them their table was ready, and Sally stood up and followed the waiter in. Nikko, walking behind her, was aware that she was relaxed now, and that, carefully handled, she would talk. He looked at her as she walked elegantly ahead of him, and his mind was a mixture of pride and pleasure in being her escort, and calculation on the conversation that they had had, and that was to come. He was aware that he was no longer thinking of her purely professionally, and he wasn't sure if that was a good thing or not. It made the evening more pleasant, however, and maybe reduced the overheads on the meal, if you looked at it that way.

CHAPTER TEN

The inside of Wheeler's was quiet and pleasant. There was a thick, dark red carpet on the floor which absorbed the sound; the walls were panelled in a light brown wood, and here and there were eighteenth-century prints in gold frames. The tables were well separated, and covered with white cloths on which the glass and cutlery sparkled. There was the muted sound of conversation and the lighting was unobtrusive: altogether, the place was very pleasant and relaxing.

Sally sat down, looking about her with satisfaction and an observant eye, since she would have to report back to Gran at headquarters, who would want to know every detail. Theirs was a small, round table at the far end of the room, and Nick sat opposite her with his back to the rest of the diners, so that she had a perfect view of everything that went on, while he had a perfect view of her.

Choosing the meal occupied them for the next few minutes. Steak and fish were the specialities of the house, but Sally wanted something a bit out of the ordinary, and steak sounded too mundane, whatever adjective was added to it, while she ate fish too often at home to want it here. She pored over the other things on the menu, asking Nikko what they were when she hadn't heard of them before, and finally settled on Chicken Maryland, not because she was mad about chicken, but she liked the idea of all that fruit. Nikko chose Steak Tartare, and they both ordered melon to start with.

'How about wine?' Nikko asked when the waiter had departed with their order.

'I haven't the head for it, not after sherry,' Sally said. She was afraid it would make her sleepy, and then she wouldn't be able to take back a full and detailed report.

Nikko, on the other hand, wanted her to be relaxed and was determined that she should have wine, so he said, 'One glass won't hurt you. You don't have to drink more if you don't want to.'

'I wouldn't drink more if I didn't want to,' Sally said with a hint of her old sharpness.

'I know,' Nikko grinned engagingly. 'You're a very determined creature when you want.' He beckoned to the wine waiter and ordered a bottle of burgundy, and then settled down to conversation again.

'So do you like hotel work, Sally?' He gave her an opening.

'Oh yes – except for obstreperous guests like you, of course,' she smiled. 'But I enjoy it, yes. It's hard work of course.'

'It must be – and you never have any time off?'

'Oh, I have a couple of hours through the day and a little while in the evenings. I don't need more, really.'

'What do you mean?'

'Well, as long as I can have a swim every day – when the weather's reasonable – and can read a chapter of my book before I go to bed, I'm happy. I wouldn't have anything to do with more spare time. I like to keep working.'

The wine arrived, and Nikko waited until Sally had tasted and approved it before he spoke again. Then he said, 'You're very much like your grandmother, aren't you?'

'In what way? To look at?'

'In character. You both believe hard work is the best antidote for trouble. But you know, it isn't good to do anything to excess. Too much work is as bad for you as too much lazing around.' He smiled at her. 'I should know – I've done both.'

'I can imagine that,' Sally said, raising an eyebrow. 'You look like the sort of person to go to extremes.'

'Ah, the gypsy looks – I've had to live up to them all my life. Really, you know, I'm a very ordinary, home-loving kind of bloke, but because I look like a pirate, I'm always having to behave like one.'

'I don't believe a word of it, so it's no good trying to play on my sympathies,' Sally said, laughing at him.

'All right, but it's true that I used to go to extremes, and it's true that I've learnt my lesson from it. You see, when you're freelance, there's no paid holidays, no sick-pay, no pay during idle times when there's no news to be had. You have to work like stink while you can to lay up enough money to keep you when you can't.'

'It must be wearing, that kind of life.'

'It is – but it's fun too. Never boring at least. But I've learnt now to regulate my life a bit more. I do some regular feature work so that I've always got some money coming in during the slack times. I'm working on a novel too, in the vague hopes that I might make it in two worlds. And I take a holiday when I've been working too hard.'

'And that's what brought you down here?'

'That's what brought me down here. And that's what I'm saying to you – that you should take time off now and then to do other things. You shouldn't let yourself get too narrow, especially when you're so young.'

Sally stirred uneasily.

'I get so restless when I'm not working. I start thinking, and I don't like that.'

'Thinking? About him?' Nikko asked, very gently. He held his breath for a moment, but no storm broke.

'Mainly. Oh, not in the way you're thinking – I mean, I don't pine for him, or grieve or anything like that, though of course I miss him.' She looked up and Nikko nodded sympathetically. Then she hesitated, as if she wasn't sure whether to go on or not. Nikko prompted her, still gently.

'What then?'

'It's silly, really, but—' Another pause. 'I have these dreams, you see. About him – about Jim. I dream that he's still alive. It makes me restless.' She stopped then, and looked at him for inspiration, or for a cue, and he said, a little puzzled as to the trend of her remarks, 'You don't believe he is still alive, do you?'

'I don't know. But the thing is, I don't know that he's dead, and it makes me restless – not to know, I mean.'

At that moment the waiter arrived with their food, and they didn't speak until he had gone and they had picked up their forks.

'Sally, what do you mean, you don't know that he's dead. There was never any doubt about it, was there?' Nikko asked.

'His body was never found. Someone saw him dive overboard, and that was all. He dived in to try and save my uncle, you see, who went over when the lifeboat was thrown against the cargo ship.'

'But surely, if he has never been heard of since, isn't that enough proof that he is dead?'

'I don't know,' Sally said, frowning down at her plate. 'You hear stories enough of people believed to be missing who turn up years later.'

'Yes, but only during the war – or when they've been lost in a jungle or something, where they couldn't get back to civilization easily. This was in the English Channel, for heaven's sake. He'd only have to get to a telephone or a police station.'

'I know it sounds silly—' Sally began, and Nikko broke in firmly, 'It certainly does. You've no evidence at all, except for a dream—'

'There is something else.'

A pause, and Nikko looked at her doubtfully. She felt unreasonably determined to convince him that it wasn't entirely silly, and she went on earnestly, 'When my uncle went overboard, the same bump that threw him over trapped a young seaman – Peter Westernra was his name – between the two vessels. That was on the opposite side from where my uncle went over, you see.' Nikko nodded. 'They got a rope round him under his arms, and pulled him up, but there was some time, a few minutes or so, when he was hanging there, half in and half out of the boat, looking in the other direction from everyone else.'

'Yes, go on. What did he see then?' Sally grimaced at him, not liking her story to be anticipated like that.

'He was brought in to me, terribly injured – dying in fact. I was nursing him, you understand, no-one else. He came round and talked to me for a bit, and he said, he said that there was a second boat on the scene, and that he saw Jim being taken on board her.'

Sally stopped, and Nikko waited as if he expected something more. It was a little piece of theatricality, for he knew that she had finished, but he wanted to make little of her evidence.

'And that's all? Sally, a dying man, probably feverish, in pain, says he saw your Jim being pulled up into a boat which in the first place wasn't there, and in the second place he couldn't have seen if it was—'

'No, listen,' Sally said angrily. 'In the first place, Peter wasn't feverish, and he wasn't in pain.'

'You said he was terribly injured.'

'So he was. He had, amongst other things, a broken back, which meant he couldn't feel anything. He was under sedation as well. He wasn't in pain. He was dying of haemorrhage – he was bleeding to death in fact. It makes you sleepy. It doesn't make you feverish.'

'Even so—'

'Let me finish. In the second place, the ship's cox said to me at the time that there could have been a dozen ships on the scene and they wouldn't have known, the weather conditions were so bad. Peter was facing the other way from everyone else. Out at sea in those conditions the visibility changes from minute to minute. It could easily be that at that moment the weather lifted enough for Peter to see the boat which had been hidden from them all a moment before.'

Nikko took time now to think before he spoke, and they ate in silence for a moment. Then he said, calmly, 'All right. Even if you accept that it might be possible, there are still some objections. If another boat picked him up, and he was alive, why didn't they take him straight back to shore to hospital? And if he was dead, why didn't they report it? One way or the other, you'd have heard, at the most a couple of days later. Besides, it's all nonsense. There was no other boat there.'

'How can you be so sure,' Sally retorted, 'you weren't even there.'

'I was there,' Nikko dropped his bombshell calmly. 'I was in a helicopter, taking photographs.'

Sally stared at him in astonishment, and had nothing to say, nothing at all.

The waiter came to clear away their first course, and when he had gone Nikko resumed.

'I managed to cadge a seat in the rescue helicopter that was sent out. We couldn't get near enough, because of the weather, to be of any help. But I had a telephoto lens on my camera, and every time the weather cleared for a moment I took a picture. I took dozens of pictures of the whole rescue. There was no other boat, Sally.'

'Did you look for one?' Sally asked after a moment.

'What d'you mean? Of course I didn't.'

'I mean that you maybe haven't studied all the photos you took. You may have missed it. It might be on the edge of a photo and you trimmed it off. If you weren't looking for another boat, you probably wouldn't have noticed one.'

'There was no other boat! Stop being such a little ass.'

'Maybe I will if you stop being such a pompous pig!'

For a moment they stared angrily at each other, until Nikko realized that it was perfectly silly to quarrel like this over something he cared nothing about. It didn't matter to him, did it, if she wanted to believe her wretched fiancé was still alive somewhere? After a moment he said, 'Look, the waiter's coming with our meal. Let's not spoil it with a silly quarrel.' He smiled at her, but she looked back, stony-faced. 'I want you to enjoy this evening, and I want to enjoy it myself'

'How can you enjoy an evening with an idiot?'

'Oh, come on, Sally, don't keep it up. Listen, I'll tell you what I'll do. I'll show you all those pictures I took from the helicopter. I'll make big prints of all of them, and we'll go over them together – with a magnifying glass if you want – and if there's any sign of another boat there, I'll believe you. And if there isn't, you'll believe me when I say it's nonsense. Is that on?'

'All right,' Sally said at last.

'Bargain?'

'It's a bargain.'

The waiter put down their plates and began to serve the vegetables. While Sally's attention was thus engaged Nikko quietly topped up the wine glasses, and when the waiter had left them again he lifted his glass to her and said, 'Here's to us, and a pleasant evening.'

Sally, not wishing to be ungenerous, lifted her glass too, and they clinked, and drank.

'And now,' Nikko said, setting down his glass, 'let's talk about something else, shall we?'

'All right, Nicky,' Sally said sweetly, 'we'll talk about you instead.'

Nikko laughed. 'You said that so menacingly. It's a pity this isn't war-time – you'd have made a wonderful Mata Hari.' Then he paused, remembering – 'You called me Nick.'

'Did I? Well, what's wrong with that?'

'That's the first time you've called me anything.'

'Do you mind "Nick"?'

'Not at all. Hardly anyone calls me that, so it will make it special.'

Nikko smiled at her across the table, and for a moment she thought how handsome he looked, with his firm brown skin, his dark curly hair, his teeth showing very white as he smiled, and his dark eyes glowing at her, reflecting the lamplight. It would be nice, she thought, to touch his hair, to be held in his strong arms – then she pulled herself up abruptly. What was she thinking of! All the same, it was nice to be taken out by a man again, and she was proud to be seen with him; and ten minutes later as she laughed at something he had said, she thought, Gran was right, he is good company, when he forgets to put on an act.

They drove back to Pengarth at about ten-thirty, wrangling happily about economics, and whether holiday camps did more harm than good to an environment, and whether there was any truth in the old sayings about the weather, and other like subjects. They parted at the door friends, having arranged to go up to Town on Monday to look at the photographs, and to meet before breakfast the next day for a swim.

The following day, at around eleven-thirty, Nikko telephoned the *Courier* offices and spoke to Ted Cooper, to arrange for a dark-room to be available for him on Monday.

'Oh, that'll be no problem, I'll fix it for you. Something on?' Cooper said.

'Might be. Can't tell yet,' Nikko hedged.

'Cagey devil. What is it, the Trevose girl still?'

'Sort of.'

'Making headway with her?'

'Yes, I'm at the boarding house now.'

'Oh, I see, can't talk now, eh? Well, don't worry, leave it to Uncle Ted. I'll have the darkest, most secluded dark-room made ready according to your special instructions, complete with settee, record-player—'

'Look, we're coming up on business,' Nikko said, breaking into his burbling.

'Don't get your rag out, son. Nikko baby, I think you're in love.'

'Oh shut up,' Nikko said, and put down the phone.

CHAPTER ELEVEN

Nikko still had the red Escort, so they were to drive up. This time Sally had decided to bear some part of the expense, and she was going to insist on buying them both lunch when the time came, for since Friday night they had not quarrelled when they had met, and she was feeling rather kindly towards him. She was excited, too, at the thought that she might at least find something out, one way or the other. It was not, she told herself often and often, that she believed Jim was still alive. It was just the uncertainty – she wanted facts, she wanted something definite.

Nikko was torn between hoping there would be some evidence on Sally's side and hoping – and being sure – that there would not be. If there was evidence, there would be a nice little mystery, and maybe a story to be got out of it. If there was not, it would put Sally back on the market, so to speak – beyond that he was not prepared to let himself think.

It was a fine day, with some cloud about, and a brisk little wind. Sally wore a dark skirt with a green blouse and a green scarf tied round her hair, and they drove with the windows down and their elbows stuck out into the rush of air. The wind stirred fronds of Sally's hair, and Nikko screwed up his eyes against the glare. Each glanced at the other from time to time, but they spoke little. They stopped early for a pub lunch, and Sally paid without too much opposition from Nikko, and then they drove on. They still didn't talk much, for they were both a little tense, a little nervous, for not entirely different reasons. It was just after one when Nikko pulled up in the side-street that ran down beside the *Courier* buildings.

'Everyone will be out at lunch,' he said.

'Does that matter?' asked Sally.

'All the better,' Nikko said. 'We can get on with it in peace. Come on.'

He led her in through a side door, and up several flights of stone steps, and then through a swing door into some corridors. Through another door, and they were in an incredibly untidy office, with a table down the middle and filing cabinets all round the walls, and every surface invisible under heaps of papers and other office rubble. The windows were so dirty it looked as if there was a thick fog outside, and the floor looked as though it hadn't been swept since the place was first built.

A young man was looking for something in a filing cabinet, and he looked up as Nikko came in.

'Hullo, Nikko. Want something?'

'Hullo Bill. Just some negs of mine. Why aren't you at lunch?'

'Panic on,' Bill said laconically. 'Some old josser's just died and we can't find anything in the morgue about him. I'm just trying to find a pic.'

'Who is it?'

'Bloke called Arthur William Billingley.'

'Billingsley,' Nikko corrected. 'Ex-councillor. I remember him. He was the one who kicked up all the stink when they wanted to run the new motorway across Eightacre Common. Got up such a hoo-ha they re-routed it two miles further north. Saved the common from destruction, the preservationists' patron saint he was. Anti-blood-sports campaigner too, funnily enough. The two don't usually go together, not in farming country. Lived over Pedhampton way. You want to look up that motorway business – '68 it was, I think.'

'Boy, I wish I had your memory, Nikko. Thanks a lot,' the young man said fervently, while Sally looked at Nikko with increased respect. Nikko meanwhile had gone over to a grey metal cupboard and opened it. To Sally's surprise, order reigned inside with as much supremacy as chaos outside – yellow boxes and packets were stacked neatly, each labelled with a white label and clear black printing. Nikko ran his hand over a couple of stacks and finally drew out a box.

'This is the one. Come on, Sally, let's get to it. I'm in the basement if anyone wants me, Bill.'

'Okay. Cheers!'

They went back into the corridor, and turned the other way and went down some dark stairs, wooden this time, into the basement where there were several dark rooms. On one of them a card was pinned with Nikko's name on it.

'This is it,' he said. 'Good old Ted.'

'Who's Ted?'

'The chap who fixed it up for me. Salt of the earth. Very reliable and all that.' He pushed open the door and put on the light. 'All set up, too, very good work.'

Sally kept out of the way and watched, fascinated, as Nikko took out the negative and set it into the enlarger, got the packet of paper ready, still in its protective box, poured the chemicals into the trays on the side table.

'Anything interesting we'll make a print of,' he explained. 'Some you'll see straight away won't help you.'

'You sound almost as if you hope there will be something,' Sally said.

'I almost do,' Nikko smiled. 'Right, lights out, let's begin.'

The red light made them both look ghastly, purple-lipped and bloated like drowned corpses, but they didn't notice that. Sally stood beside him as he switched on the light in the enlarger and adjusted the first negative until it was in focus.

'Not much to see here,' Nikko said, making the image larger. 'They'll be in the order I took them, of course, since they're still in reel form. We never used any of these. I was furious.'

They went through them one by one, and took prints of four. The prints were laid in the developer, and Sally stood by the dish, fascinated as she watched the picture appear and darken like magic. Then they were rinsed, put into the fixer, and rinsed again, and then at last the light could go on and Sally could have a proper look at them.

'Too dark,' Nikko said. 'The trouble is, they're dark negs, so we'll have to be careful if we lighten them. I'll do another batch a bit lighter and a bit bigger. Just these three. I don't think this one will be any good.'

The lights went off again, and three more prints were made, the developing-rinsing-fixing routine repeated, and then with the lights on the prints carefully inspected. Nikko took a glass like a jeweller's eye-piece and held up the prints one by one, going over them at close quarters. He was just about to put the third one down, when he hesitated, bringing it back close to his eye.

'What is it?' Sally asked.

'I don't know. I'm going to blow this one up as far as it will go.'

Off lights. Sally watched, mystified, as a new print was taken of one corner only of the original negative. She felt vaguely excited, but didn't know why. On lights. Nikko held up the new print, still dripping, and examined it. Then he gave a sharp cry of discovery, snatched up his eye-glass again, and looked closely through it.

'What is it?' Sally asked anxiously. 'Nick, what have you found?'

But he would not be hurried. At length he laid the print down flat on the table, smoothing it flat with a cloth. The picture had been blown up so far that it became grainy, and at first look it was just a messy blur; but Nikko looked at Sally proudly, and pointed to one corner. 'There,' he said. 'Look at that.'

A dark smudge, that was all Sally saw. She looked at Nikko enquiringly.

'Stand back a bit, get the impression of light and shade; narrow your eyes a bit. See it now?'

'Ye-es,' Sally said doubtfully, and then sharply, 'Yes! It's the prow of a boat.'

'Right! And look here, and here, you can see the line of the gunwale through the spray.'

'Yes, you're right! You can't see it at first, it looks just like more water. But it's a boat all right.'

'Good. Now take the glass, and look at the prow closely.' Sally obeyed, focusing on the darker triangle in the greyness. 'What do you see?'

'Little white marks – of course! The boat's name and port!' She straightened up, flushed with excitement. 'Nick, we were right, there was another boat. No-one could doubt it now.'

'You were right, Sally. I apologize profusely for doubting you.'

'Don't be silly,' she dismissed his apologies. 'But listen, can we blow it right up so's we can read the name?'

Nikko shook his head slowly, sad to disappoint her.

'I'm afraid not. You see how grainy it is already. If I raised it any more it would just be a lot of dots. You couldn't read it.'

Sally looked stricken. 'Oh but you must! You can't leave it now, now you've got so far. Try, please try.'

'I'll do one for you, but it won't be any good, you'll see.'

'Try all the same.'

'All right, but I'll have to get another enlarger.'

He was right, of course. After a lengthy process the enlargement appeared, and was, as he predicted, completely indecipherable. Sally stared at it until her eyes ached, hoping to make something out, but in the end she had to admit defeat, and she put the print down with a groan.

'How absolutely maddening,' she said. 'To get so near—'

'Well, look on the bright side. You've learnt more than you ever expected to learn. You do at least know that there was a boat.'

'As Peter said. And if he was right about that, he could have been right about Jim being taken up on it.'

'It's possible,' Nikko said grudgingly. 'Just.'

'Oh, don't be so mean about it,' Sally exclaimed.

'I'm not being mean, Sally, but remember it must have been some way off. How could he have recognized Jim at that distance?'

'Well, he might have. But what puzzles me is, if the boat was as clear as this, why didn't any of the crew see it?'

'They were at sea-level, remember. I was looking down from above. The crew were probably half-blinded with spray.'

'Um,' Sally said absently. She was studying the earlier print, looking at the outline of the boat. 'Now you know it's here, it's quite plain to be seen,' she said. 'You know, the outline isn't familiar. I don't think she's a British vessel.'

'How can you tell?'

'Well, you can see by her size she's a fishing boat of some sort, and she doesn't look like our fishing boats. I wonder—'

She paused in thought for a long time, and seeing her preoccupied, Nikko busied himself with clearing up. He marked the relevant negative in the roll, and restored the roll to its box, emptied the chemical trays, put the box of paper back in the drawer, pulled out the plug and rolled up the flex neatly. Then Sally exclaimed, 'Frenchy!'

'What?'

'Frenchy Polwheal! He's the one who'll know.'

'Stop being mysterious and tell me,' Nikko demanded.

'He's one of the lifeboat crew, a shocking, disreputable old scoundrel. He used to be notorious for smuggling – that's why they called him Frenchy of course – and if there's anything a bit crooked or shady going on in the village, you can bet Frenchy's at the bottom of it.'

'Smuggling? In this day and age? Come on, Sally, you've been reading too many comics.'

'There you go again,' Sally said contemptuously, 'thinking you know everything. There's more smuggling now than ever before. Everything from spirits to illegal immigrants. You don't know the half of it!'

'All right, even if there is, what's this got to do with our little mystery?'

'Well, I was thinking to myself, if there was another boat, and we know now that there was, why didn't she come forward and try to help? Instead of skulking about in the mist like that? It didn't seem reasonable, unless she had some good reason for not getting herself spotted. And why shouldn't she want to be seen? Because she shouldn't have been there, because she was doing something illegal?'

'Possibly. Go on,' Nikko said, unconvinced.

'Say she was smuggling, running in under cover of the storm? Came on the rescue scene, didn't want to give herself away unless it was absolutely essential, hung about, and helped to the extent of picking up a man overboard? Well then, if anyone like Frenchy did happen to spot her, he wouldn't say anything about it, because it would be in his own interests to keep quiet, wouldn't it?'

Nikko nodded, and then said, 'All right, supposing. But in the first place, no ship would be lunatic enough to put to sea in a storm like that.'

'Well, obviously not, but they might have put to sea in a bit of a storm, and it got worse on them. It's been known to happen.'

'All right, but even so, if they did pick up Jim, why didn't they report it?'

'They wouldn't, not to the police. Of course they wouldn't. Smugglers don't go near the police voluntarily. They'd just—'

A silence. Nikko prompted her. 'Yes?'

'Yes, I see,' she said at last. 'I do see. You mean, if they did pick him up, he would have to be dead, otherwise he would have reported back.'

Another silence, and then she sighed. 'Well, you know, I didn't really think they picked him up alive. But it was the not knowing, you see.'

They made their way up from the basement and back to the room where Nikko put away the negatives.

Sally was preoccupied, and Nikko, thinking she was upset, said gently, 'Would you like to go and have a drink?'

'What? Oh, no, we must get back,' she said, sounding eager again. 'The trouble is, you'll have to do this part of it – I could never pump him successfully.'

'Pump who? What are you talking about?'

'Frenchy, of course. You're good at wheedling stories out of people, aren't you? Well, here's a chance to show all your skills. Find out what boat it was and where she came from. And if he really doesn't know, find out where smuggling boats come from on that side. He must know. It'll probably be a little harbour, as small as Pengarth or even smaller. The larger ones would be patrolled too well.'

'What are you talking about now?' Nikko said, exasperated.

'You can get him in the pub tonight. Buy him a drink or something – you'll know best how to go about it. But we must know at least the name of the port, or some ports, to narrow down the search.'

'Search for what?'

'For Jim.' She saw him about to protest, and forestalled

him. 'Oh, I know he can't be alive, I know that, don't worry. But I have to know where they buried him. I can't rest until I know for certain. You see that, don't you?'

'I'm beginning to,' Nikko said grimly.

CHAPTER TWELVE

Nikko was not entirely unhappy at having been cast in the role of private investigator, but he was a little worried, not having the slightest idea of how to go about extracting the information he wanted. He was very silent on the drive back, for the more he thought about it and turned it over in his mind, the more he felt there was no adequate reason for this old smuggler to give him what he wanted; and if he couldn't see a reason, how much less would Frenchy Polwheal!

He knew nothing of the man, moreover, except that he was a 'rum-runner' and apparently incapable of going at anything straight, and a magnificent sailor. Sally had shown him a picture, for which they had rummaged amongst back numbers for the shot taken of the lifeboat crew on the day after the disaster, but, typically, Frenchy appeared on it in profile only, as he tried to back away from the camera, and Nikko was not even sure he would recognize him.

'Oh, you'll recognize him all right,' Sally had said confidently. 'And anyway, even if you couldn't, everyone else knows him, they'd point him out. He isn't liked in the village, but they tolerate him – the other smugglers do, at least. The honest ones hate him, of course.'

So it was Nikko found himself that evening heading for the lower end of the harbour where the rougher pubs were, with plenty of money in his pocket, his camera, out of sheer habit, over his shoulder, and no plan of action in his head. It was still early to be thinking of getting anyone talking, but he wanted to prime his own pump before he started anything, and so he slipped quietly into the public bar of the Happy Return, a small and picturesque-looking pub sandwiched between two fish-stores on the West Quay.

A silence fell as he came in, and the eyes of everyone in the bar lifted and stared at him, expressionlessly. The barman came away from the person he was talking to in the corner and slid sideways up the bar until he was opposite Nikko.

'Good evening,' Nikko said quietly, smiling as pleasantly and confidently as he could.

'Evening,' the barman said, and the man he had been talking to nodded, not unpleasantly. The rest of the eyes went back to what they had been doing before.

'I'll have a pint of special, please,' Nikko said. He slid up onto a stool two down from the other man, a distance he had carefully calculated as he came in as being not too friendly and not too standoffish. It was apparently all right, for the man continued to look at him without hostility, as if waiting for him to speak.

'Been a lovely day,' Nikko said.

'Ugh,' the man assented.

'I expect the farmers could do with a drop of rain, though,' he went on.

'Ar,' the man agreed.

The barman put down Nikko's pint, and he turned to the other man and said, 'Have a drink?'

For a moment Nikko felt himself scrutinized, and then the man said, 'Thanks.'

The barman without further instruction poured a pint of some dark, flat-looking ale and slapped it down in front of the other customer with a 'S'your night, ennit, Jim?'

'How about yourself?' Nikko said to the barman.

'I'll have one later thank you sir,' he said all in one breath, rang up the price, and put some of Nikko's change up on a shelf for his 'drink later.'

Nikko looked round him as unobtrusively as possible. Apart from 'Jim' at the bar, there were four others sitting down in a corner playing euchre, three youngish men, and a greybeard, all wearing guernseys, dirty trousers, and seaboots, and a stoutish, middle-aged man in slacks and a jersey alternately making comments on their play and throwing darts in a practising kind of way at the dart-board. None of them looked disreputable enough to be in any way connected with Frenchy Polwheal. Still, it was early yet.

107

'Holiday?' the barman asked him, picking up a glass and polishing it with professional dexterity.

'Not really,' Nikko said. 'Just snatching a few days. I shouldn't be here really, but who's to know?'

The barman smiled politely, and the other man, Jim, nodded his head towards Nikko's camera.

'Thassa fancy-looking job you got there. You'd be a bit of an expert, I'd say.'

'Yes, it's a nice little job, this one,' Nikko said, lifting the camera and holding it up so that Jim could see it properly. 'It's my favourite – light enough to carry, but it knows a few tricks.'

'Professional, encha?'

'Yes, how did you know?'

'Ar,' said Jim, rubbing his nose knowingly.

'Newspaper?' the barman asked, and his voice had an edge to it that made Nikko nervous.

'No, not really. I do illustrations for magazines, that kind of thing.'

'Not a reporter, then?' the barman asked.

'God, no!' Nikko laughed. 'I couldn't even write a letter home! No, pictures is my line. Illustrations, postcards, birthday cards, even Christmas cards. Anything that'll make a good picture—'

The barman gave a quick glance at one of the seated group, and Nikko was aware of a relaxing amongst the company, and he realized with a quickening of his pulse that there was something here to be got at. They had been worried about him being a reporter, and why else than that they had something to hide, something they didn't want getting into the papers? Well, he had got somewhere. At least he knew now he was in the right pub. He would get himself well in here, and then later he might have the chance to force an introduction through these men to the one he wanted.

For a while he chatted to Jim and the barman about the weather, and farming, and the latest headlines – at least, he called it chatting, but it was all very laconical and Jim's comments were so brief they almost sounded like telegrams. However he felt no dislike in them, and the barman was friendly enough. When Jim came to the end of his pint he nodded to them both and said he must be going, and in the doorway he passed an old man and woman coming in. The barman went down the bar to serve them with a cheery greeting, and Nikko strolled casually over to the euchre group, and after watching for a minute or two, said to the fifth man, 'Fancy a game of darts?'

For a moment Nikko felt himself being scrutinized by all five, and then the man said, 'Don't mind. Three-oh-one?'

'Whatever you usually play, I don't mind,' Nikko said. 'Do they have any darts at the bar?'

'Here,' said one of the seated men, a round, fair, rosy-faced man who looked as though he couldn't have done anyone a bad turn if he tried, 'you can borrow mine, s'long's you don't drop 'em.' From under the table he produced a long box containing a set of long-stemmed, feather flighted darts that Nikko was almost afraid to take, they looked so expensive and well-cared-for.

'Thanks a lot,' he said, wondering at the generosity.

'You c'n leave your camra here – I'll watch it for you,' said the man, and for a moment Nikko hesitated, hating to entrust his camera to anyone, before he realized that it was the security demanded against the loan of the darts.

'Okay thanks,' he said, trying to sound as easy about it as possible. The man took the camera and put it on the ledge under the table, and Nikko was relieved to find that he could at least see it where it was. He had been afraid it would disappear completely.

They went through the ritual of throwing for first off and chalker, and Nikko lost.

'On holiday, are you?' the man asked as he toed the line for his first throw. The three darts thumped the board, no double.

'Well, sort of – call it a working holiday,' Nikko said, taking his place. His third dart found the double thirteen. 'Twenty-six away,' he said, going up to chalk it.

'Working holiday?' the man queried.

'I'm a photographer. Illustrations, postcards, that sort of

thing. Plenty to snap round here, I must say,' he added, making it sound like a personal compliment to the man.

'I daresay,' he said, getting away with a double eighteen, and following it up with a twenty and a one. 'Fifty-seven up.'

'Leave off, Arnie – no practisin'!' the young man at the euchre table called in cheerful mockery, and then added to Nikko, 'You 'ave to watch Arnie – 'e cheats like stinko if you let 'im.'

'Thanks for the tip,' Nikko grinned. 'The name's Nick, by the way.'

'Pleasetermeetcha,' the young man said. 'I'm Will, an' thass Charlie, Arnie, Fin, an' Spinney.'

'Pleased to meet you,' Nikko said, and round the group they nodded and murmured to him, a qualified welcome. 'That's a fascinating game to watch,' Nikko went on. 'Damned if I can tell what you're doing at all.'

'Foreigners never can,' said Charlie with a mixture of pride and spite.

'Wanterwatch them,' Arnie said, taking his next throw. 'They'd 'ave the shirt orf yer back iffn you sat down at euchre with 'em. See that notice?'

He gestured towards the bar as he went up to collect his darts. Nikko looked across and saw a large, highly-coloured, home-made poster stuck on the mirror behind the bar. It read, 'No Euchre To Be Played In This Bar – by order.'

Nikko turned back and raised an eyebrow in enquiry. The man called Spinney gathered the cards in, squared them with a slap, and dealt again, giving a mild titter at the same time.

'That were the last guv'nor, before Jack Hills took over. They was a chap in here was a euchre king – Frenchy was 'is name – and 'e used to make a fair old living in the summer teaching the foreigners euchre. In the end 'e was makin' more money outen 'em than the guv'nor. He took so much orf 'em, they couldn't afford to buy no beer. So 'e puts up the notice – no euchre to be played.'

He stopped and tittered again. Nikko took his throw quickly so as not to miss the end of the story – at last he had heard the name Frenchy.

'So what happened then?' he asked.

110

'Wuss thing 'e ever did fer 'imself,' Spinney went on. 'We all went on strike, sort of – wouldn't come in no more – we went down the Spotted Calf. All 'e 'ad in was the foreigners, and ole Frenchy.'

'Frenchy still came in?'

'Course he did.' Will took up the story, laughing. 'He stopped playing euchre, and started teaching the foreigners "Twenty-five". Said it never made no difference to him. Said if the guv'nor banned Twenty-five, he'd start on Hundred-and-One.'

'Well, 'e wore down the old guv'nor all right,' said Spinney. 'That an' the fact we wasn't none of us drinkin' in 'ere. Th'ole guv'nor left, and Jack Hills took over. Jack had the right idea. He didn't ban euchre – he banned Frenchy.'

The whole company laughed at this conclusion to the story, and Nikko remembered how Sally had said Frenchy was tolerated, but not liked. The germ of an idea started to grow in his mind.

Nikko finished his game with Arnie, beating him on a good three-dart finish that was mostly luck, but which he contrived to carry off as skill, and since Arnie seemed disinclined for a return match, Nikko asked the company in general if anyone wanted a game.

'Tell you what, why don't you sit down an' we'll teach you euchre?' Will said, laughing. Glancing round, and seeing that no-one in particular was against it, Nikko said, 'So long as you let me keep my shirt.'

'Thass orl right, young'un,' Spinney said genially. 'I lay you've got enough money to get through the night. Sit you down nexter Charlie there.'

'I'll just get a drink in first,' Nikko said, and asked round the table, 'what is it?'

Will and Fin were drinking light-and-bitter, and the other three were drinking something called 'Owl' which turned out to be locally brewed mild, the darkish, flat-looking beer he had seen poured out for the man at the bar. He bought the round in, and then sat down, feeling very much accepted by them. He was sure that by the end of the evening he would be well enough in to find out what he wanted.

The fishermen were canny, however, and any time he managed to bring up anything to do with smuggling, even the remotest hint, they would dexterously slide round it, and he had to be careful to avoid arousing their suspicions. In the end, when they had been playing for some time, and Nikko was at last holding his own against the wily local experts, he came at the subject another way. Will asked why Nikko had decided to come to Pengarth in the first place, and he answered, 'Well, to tell you the truth, it was because I felt I'd missed out on something.'

'How d'you mean?'

'Well, I read all about the storm you had here last year, and I saw the pictures in the papers, and I thought, if only I'd gone down there, I could have got a whole lot better pictures than the goon who took these. This was the day after, you understand, that the pictures were taken. Of course in an emergency you don't expect good pictures – and to tell you the truth, most of these newspaper boys don't know a good picture from a hole in the wall.' He stressed the idea that he was not connected with newspapers because of their earlier hostility to the idea.

'Well, anyway, I saw the pictures they took, and I decided I'd get down here by hook or by crook, because I knew there was some great material here to be photographed. But, what with one thing and another, I never made it. Too much else to do.' He played a card, and then said casually, 'That was a sad business, wasn't it?'

'Ar. But you expect to lose a man now and then,' Fin said philosophically.

'Are any of you lifeboat men?' Nikko asked.

'All of us,' Will answered. 'Spinney there's the cox.'

'Really? That's interesting. Then you must have been out that night? The night the two men were lost?'

'Spinney was, and Fin and Arnie,' Will said. 'I was away, down in Portsmouth, and Charlie, he wasn't fit. Bloke what went over, he was only a stand-in. Damn shame really, but we was three men short that night.'

'If I'd been out, 'stead of Fred Trevose, he'd still have been alive today,' Charlie said gloomily. 'And young Jim too.'

'Now Charlie, no call to talk like that,' Spinney said in the kind of voice that revealed it was not the first time he had said it.

'Well, the fact remains, if Fred hadn't stood in for me, he wouldn't have gone over, and young Jim wouldn't have gone in after him.'

'For that matter,' Will broke in cheerfully, 'if Arnie hadn't had to stand in for me, he could've stood in for you. But you don't catch me crying into me beer about it. These things happen, Char. He might've stayed at home and fallen downstairs next day and broke his neck.'

'It's easy enough for you to talk—' Charlie began, half resentful at having his dramatic role usurped in this cavalier manner, but Will cut him off, a little less genially.

'Yes, well shut up about it, eh? Whose round is it, anyway? Fin?'

'No, 's Charlie's round. Gettinem in, Char?'

Charlie got up, muttering under his breath, and fetched a round. They waited for him in silence, and when he finally sat down again, it seemed that the topic was not yet dead. Spinney said at last, 'It's that young girl I feel sorry for. Thass a hard thing for a youngster. Good little maid she is too.'

'She's got over it all right,' Fin said, possibly to avoid adding fuel to Charlie's lachrymose fire, but Will said, scornfully, 'Looks like it, doanit? She never stops working from morning till night. Her and her Granny both. There's two women don't want to stop to think.'

'Good luck to 'em,' Arnie said. 'Women mostly don't work enough. Sit about all day pettin' 'emselves up, making a big thing outen a toothache, bitter hard work's all they need.'

'Isn't a family these parts has given so much to this village as the Trevoses,' Spinney said. 'That young Sally's another of 'em. Just wish there was something we could do for them, to make up.'

The subject was changed then, but the outburst from Charlie and the sad contemplation of the Trevose tragedy seemed to have put a damper on the evening, and shortly afterwards Spinney announced that he had better be getting,

113

and the group broke up. Nikko said cheerful goodbyes to everyone and promised to look in again, and managed to slide out alongside Spinney and keep up with him as the old man marched rapidly away down the quay. Nikko hurried and fell in beside him, and Spinney gave him a glance of momentary surprise, quickly followed by an expression of shrewdness.

'What you after, son? You a snooper?'

'A what?' Nikko asked, startled.

'You're after some'at,' Spinney said, striding on, looking straight ahead. 'You been poking and prying about, trying to wheedle some'at out of us. What you after? You police?'

'No, of course not. But you're right, I am after something.' Nikko decided to come out into the open. 'Is there somewhere we could talk – private?'

Spinney stopped abruptly and turned to look at Nikko, arms akimbo, his beard jutting forward and his mouth set with a mixture of cunning and humour.

'There ent nowhere privater than the open air, you should learn that son. Indoors, folks could be hiding behind every door, listening in on you. Out here, no-one couldn't get near enough to hear without you'd see 'em first. Come on, out with it. What you want to know?'

'That night you were out in the lifeboat – the night the two men went over – there was another boat at the scene of the rescue. It was a French boat, maybe fishing, maybe smuggling. I want to know her name and port, that's all.'

'Now why should you think there was another boat there?' Spinney asked. Nikko got the feeling that he wasn't prevaricating, but just wanted to find out how much Nikko really knew.

'Two people saw her; one person photographed her.' Spinney, confronted by firm evidence, nodded.

'Well, supposin'. Why didn't she come to the rescue? If there was a boat on hand, she'd 'a tried to help, surely?'

'You'd have thought so. That's why we reckoned she must have been where she shouldn't have been – didn't want to draw attention to herself. So we naturally thought she was either fishing outside her limits, or smuggling.'

'Who's we?'

Nikko hesitated a moment, weighing up the advantages and disadvantages in his mind, and then admitted, 'Sally Trevose.' There was a silence, while Spinney did some considering, and then Nikko went on, 'Listen, I don't want anyone to get into trouble. Nobody has to admit anything. Maybe nobody else saw this boat. All I want to know is, if there was a boat there, where did she come from, and who might she be? A person might be able to give a very good guess at that, without necessarily having been involved in anything illegal.'

Another silence, and then out of the gathering dusk came the sound of Spinney's creaky laughter.

'Son, I reckon you shoulda been a detective after all. You got all the right words. Now listen,' he turned abruptly to face Nikko, suddenly businesslike, 'I never saw no boat there, but that's not to say there mightn't have been a boat. We was all that busy, we didn't have no time for sight-seein'. Any ways, if there was a boat, and if that boat was a Frenchie, and if she might have been doing something she didn't want no-one to know about, well then, she might or she might not have come from St Martins, or then she might have come from the Duke's Egglysies – who can say?'

'Thanks,' Nikko said after a brief pause, when it seemed that that was all he was going to get. Spinney nodded, and was about to turn away when he paused and said, 'I known Sally since she first fell into the harbour, when she was only two. She shoulda come to me straight. You tell her that.'

'I'll tell her,' Nikko said, smiling.

Spinney stumped away up the quay, and Nikko was suddenly struck with a thought. He called out in a half whisper, 'Spinney?' The old man stopped and turned his head. 'What *was* she running?'

'Brandy, mostly,' the whisper came back through the dusk. Nikko smiled. The old man lifted a hand, and went on his way.

CHAPTER THIRTEEN

Nikko and Sally were poring over a soundings map, spread out on one of the tables in the deserted dining-room – a kind of neutral ground where they could meet. Nikko was trying hard to concentrate on the map, but it was not easy, with Sally's coppery hair brushing his cheek and her bare brown arm against his as they leaned together, looking for the ports Spinney had mentioned.

'Well, here's St Martins, anyway – must be,' Sally said at last.

'Where?'

'Just there – no, by my thumb.'

'That's a tiny place!' Nikko exclaimed.

'Well, of course it is!' Sally exclaimed. 'You don't think they're going to smuggle out of Calais harbour, do you, with the harbour police and the douanes and everything?'

'All right, sorry. Of course they wouldn't. But where's this other place? The Duke's Thingummy?'

'I don't know,' Sally said, puzzled. 'Are you sure that's what he said? It doesn't sound like a name at all, to me. It certainly isn't French.'

'Perhaps it's a translation of the French name. I don't know. But that's what he said, all right.'

'Maybe he was pulling your leg.'

'I don't think so. He didn't sound as if he was. Look, it's probably somewhere near this St Martins place, isn't it? Well, we'll start there, and work along the coast, you go that way and I'll go this way, and see if there's anything that would translate.'

'Okay. Let's see then, um – um – um – oh!' Sally exclaimed in dawning understanding. 'Of course! That would be how he pronounced it!'

'What?'

'This little port here – it's called Les Deux Eglises – the two churches.'

'I see,' Nikko began to laugh. 'He pronounced it the way it was spelt – hence his Dukes Egglysies.'

'It's about ten miles from St Martins by sea – more like twenty by road, I should think, and there's nothing in between them. It must all be pretty deserted round there. No wonder they took to smuggling. I should think a stranger there would stick out like a sore thumb; they wouldn't be afraid of being taken by surprise. It won't be so hard, though, if we arrive by sea. We might manage some minor damage and ask for help.'

'What are you burbling about now?' Nikko asked nervously.

'We can borrow my uncle Henry's boat. It'll be a bit rough, but the crossing will only take a day or two at the most.'

'What Uncle Henry's boat is this?'

'My Grandmother's brother, who lives at Mansell, down the coast about a mile. He's got a little dinghy and I know he wouldn't mind lending it to us. It's got a cabin and bunks and a stove and everything, so you needn't worry. And she's dead easy to handle. A child could sail her.'

'Sail her where? What are you talking about, Sally?'

'Well, what do you think I'm talking about?' Sally said, exasperated. 'We're going to borrow Uncle Henry's dinghy and sail over to St Martins and Deux Eglises and make enquiries.'

'Are we?' Nikko said, trying to sound grim.

'Well, why else did we make these enquiries? You aren't going to back out now are you? Don't tell me you're scared of sailing?'

'You can sound very arrogant when you want,' Nikko told her severely. 'One day it's going to land you in trouble.'

'I'll go on my own if you're scared, but I'd rather you came,' Sally said.

'Look, Sally, why not give this thing up? What do you hope to find out? You know he must be dead, don't you?'

'I thought I'd explained all that to you,' Sally said wearily. 'I know he's dead, but I have to be sure. I want to know who picked him up, and where they put his body. I can't

117

rest until I know. Don't you see, it would be like reading a thriller and then finding the last two pages are missing.'

'Nikko looked at her lovely, serious face, and then sighed.

'All right, if you feel you must. Naturally I'll come with you – it might be a laugh even. But what about your Gran?'

'In what way?'

'Well, firstly, can you get time off? How will she manage? And secondly, what will you tell her? She won't like you going off like that, will she?'

'I'll fix it up, don't worry,' Sally said. 'We can be over there and back in a week, and I know someone who would fill in for me for a week. I've got some money saved, and I don't mind spending that on this girl's wages. But what about you? Can you get time off?'

'That is probably the only advantage of being freelance,' Nikko said. 'You can go where you want, when you want.'

'Okay, then. I'll get to work, and I'll let you know as soon as I've got it worked out, when we're leaving.'

'All right. See you at dinner tonight. I'd better go out today and try to take some pictures I can sell. Every little helps, you know.'

Two days later, Uncle Henry's dinghy, the 'Sea Wife', was tied up to the quay in front of the Pottery, Sally having sailed it round from Mansell, and Nikko was inspecting it with mixed approval. The Sea Wife was clinker-built in the old style in darkly varnished wood, but her top-decks were painted white, and her sails were dark blue, so she was not uncolourful. She was bermuda-rigged, and inside the tiny cabin there were two bunks, a marine toilet, and a calor-gas stove. She looked sturdy and sea-worthy enough, but as to comfort, Nikko told himself he'd sooner spend a couple of nights in the nick.

'Billy Watt's lending me his outboard motor, but we'll save that for emergencies,' Sally said as she sat down to a late supper at the kitchen table, with Gran and Nikko. Nikko felt honoured to be there, for it was the first time he had been invited into the private quarters, and it seemed as though he was being accepted at last.

'Why don't we use it all the time?' Nikko wanted to know. With an engine, he thought, they could be over there in no time.

'We've limited storage space,' Sally explained. 'We can't carry much fuel for it. It isn't meant for long journeys, anyway – its only meant for getting you back in if you're really becalmed, or if you break your mast, or something like that.'

'Have you been over her thoroughly, Sally?' Gran asked, trying to conceal her anxiety.

'Yes, I have, so don't worry. We'll be back before you know it, Gran. And anyway, we'll hardly run into any rough weather at this time of year.'

'You can get rough weather any time of the year,' Gran said.

'Yes, I know, but I've had a look at the met. charts, and everything looks fine. Now, if you've finished, Nick, we'll load her up, and then we can start as soon as it gets light tomorrow. That'll be about half past three, quarter to four time.'

Nikko groaned. 'It will hardly be worth going to bed, to get up that early.'

'Suit yourself. I'll certainly be going to bed tonight,' Sally said coldly. 'If I were you, I should get an early night too.'

'Bless you, child, he was only joking,' Gran laughed at her sternness.

They carried out blankets and spare pairs of socks and jumpers and towels, wrapping them in large polythene bags and stowing them in the lockers. They took out food, tins of baked beans – the yachtsman's staple diet, it seemed to Nikko – sausages, eggs, milk, cocoa, bread, and, in case it was very hot during the day, cans of beer. Nikko, unconsciously imitating Uncle Fred's example, hid a half-bottle of whisky under the blankets just in case his nerve failed him at any time, and Sally sorted out charts and maps, and tide tables and sunset tables, and navigation equipment and lights and spare ropes and sail repair kit, and all the other essentials that Nikko wouldn't have known if he'd fallen over them in his own front room.

Last of all, after everyone else had departed to their

119

various evening tasks, Sally went back alone and stowed in a drawer under the folding table the photograph of Jim which she had resurrected from the suitcase under her bed. It was a good likeness, and it might be necessary to jog someone's memory. She took a last look round, and then went back home to bed where she slept soundly, peaceful in the knowledge that she was *doing* something at last.

They were up and washed and dressed and breakfasted in the dark before dawn. Gran, indefatigable, rose too and cooked for them, and despite the early hour they managed to put away eggs, bacon, sausages, and fried bread, as well as toast and marmalade and tea.

'Get a good meal inside you before you go. You might have to make do on scrat the rest of the day,' she said, and while they ate she cut cheese sandwiches and ham sandwiches for them to take with them.

'You don't need to bother, Gran,' Sally said when she saw what Gran was doing; but Gran said, 'You'll be hungry again by mid-morning, and you won't want to stop for food, if I know you.'

'You're right there. I want to make a landfall while it's still light. I don't fancy groping about shoals in the dark,' Sally said.

The first grey light was creeping in, and Sally pushed back her chair impatiently. 'Are you ready?' she said to Nikko, and he could hear the tremor of excitement in her voice. For that matter, he was pretty excited too, not to say nervous. In the cold light of day it seemed insane to be going out in that tiny boat, when only one of them knew anything about sailing. Still, a short life and a merry, he thought.

'I'm ready. Have we got everything?'

'All except the water,' Sally said.

'Water?' Nikko was mystified.

'Fresh water. For drinking,' Sally said, grinning at him, amused at his ignorance. I'm going to afford her plenty of opportunities for mirth of that kind, Nikko thought. 'I'll take the sandwiches, and your anorak, and you bring the drum of water. OK?'

'Okay, skipper,' Nikko said, saluting her. Gran filled the

drum and detached the hose, and Nikko took the handle and wheeled it out onto the quay, and with Sally's help and directions stowed it and attached the short hose and tap, and then came back up.

The day was calm and grey, with a good brisk little wind that ruffled his hair and flapped Gran's cardigan which she had slung round her shoulders. Sally looked about her and snuffed the air like a dog.

'It'll be hot later on. I just hope the sun doesn't suck up all the wind,' she said. She, like Nikko, was dressed in jeans and a thick sweater and plimsolls, but she took the plimsolls off at once and threw them into the cabin. 'Can't balance unless my feet are bare,' she explained. Gran up on the quayside watched gravely, as if one sea departure was the same as another to her, but Nikko could guess her anxious feelings.

'We'll be back in about a week, then, Gran. If we can get ashore anywhere decent I'll try and give you a ring, but don't worry if I don't.'

'All right, dear. Take care, won't you?'

'I will, don't worry. Bye Gran!'

'God bless you both,' Gran said, and she turned abruptly and went back into the house.

Nikko was a little surprised, but Sally said, 'She doesn't want to stand and watch us out of sight. I'd understand that.'

'Really?' Nikko was puzzled.

'Well, you see, if we didn't come back, that would be the last sight of us. She'd rather the last sight was a bit more intimate.'

Nikko shrugged, not really understanding.

'What do I do?' he asked, anxious now to be getting on with it.

'Untie the rope from the mooring line and coil it down, and then get ready to shove us off when I say,' Sally said. She rolled up the sleeves of her Arran sweater and fitted in the tiller, and then prepared to hoist the sails. At her word, Nikko, standing in the stern, shoved them off from the quayside as hard as he could, and in a moment the sails flapped once or twice, and then picked up the breeze, and they ran smoothly forward. In a few minutes they were past the bar, and as soon as they cleared the shelter of the land, the breeze seemed to stiffen, and the Sea Wife braced herself, and leaning against its strength, raced tautly forward, seeming to skim the waves. Nikko felt his spirits lift irresistibly, and Sally, having given him the sheet and settled him to trim the boat, took the tiller and grinned at him happily.

'Lovely, isn't it?'

'It's great,' Nikko smiled back at her. 'Worth getting up for.'

'It'll be hot later. You'll get lovely and brown,' she said cheerfully. 'We'll run up the coast a bit first, and then we'll head straight across. We should be running almost before the wind, and then, as long as we keep a look out for other vessels, she'll practically sail herself.'

'How far is it?' Nikko asked.

'It's about a hundred miles across, and then about another twenty along the coast the other side. With any luck at all we should make a landfall before dark.'

'That sounds like an awful long way,' Nikko said, but the novelty of the swift, free movement was so stimulating that he couldn't feel worried at the prospect.

'Nuts. It's only a hop-step-and-a-jump by sea. You'll hardly notice the time passing. Now, pay attention, we have to tack.'

The Sea Wife, as Sally had said, was easy to handle, and as they had to go about several times in the first part of the run up the coast, by the time Nikko would normally be having his breakfast he was no longer a mere passenger and knew his position for either tack, and knew what to do when they gybed.

It was all very idyllic. The sun grew hot, and they stripped off and continued in bathing costumes and tee-shirts. Nikko discarded his plimsolls as well, and Sally tied up her tangled hair into a pony-tail, so they were comfortable. They were, as Gran had predicted, starving by mid-morning, and at ten o'clock, when they were running comfortably before the wind over a moderate sea the colour of sapphires and clear to the horizon, Sally left Nikko in charge of the tiller and went below to make tea for them both.

She brought up two mugs of it, and the packets of sandwiches, and they perched side by side on the gunwale to eat.

'These taste like heaven,' Sally said.

'I've never tasted anything so good,' Nikko agreed, and he meant it.

'Funny how one always eats like a horse at sea.' A seagull that was following them, hanging idly on the wind, gave an extra flap and swooped down to perch on their prow. 'Hitch-hiker,' Sally said. The gull eyed them sideways, and preened his wings with swipes of his villainous-looking beak.

'He's after the sandwiches, I expect,' Nikko said.

'He's out of luck, then,' Sally said. 'I'm too ravenous to part with any of mine.'

The Sea Wife bounded on, giving lifts occasionally to gulls. Nikko wondered why they were so far out from land, but Sally said they hung about looking for ships, and sometimes even went right across on the ferries, and then caught the next boat back. As the sun grew hotter, the wind died down a little, and Sally trimmed the boat a little closer to the wind, and the movement of the waves became more noticeable. Nikko wondered idly if he was going to feel seasick, but he felt far too happy for it to be more than an idle wonder. The air was dazzlingly bright and breathtakingly fresh, and he felt as though he were twice as alive as he had been before. He did not tire of the movement, or of the view; the wide blue sea, the misty toy shapes of ships far away, the leech of Sea Wife's mainsail, Sally's golden skin and red-gold hair – it was all like a dream, but more real than any waking moment ever before.

By mid-day the wind had dropped so far that they were only just making enough way to steer.

'Sun's sucked it up,' Sally said. 'We'll be becalmed in half an hour.'

'What do we do then?' Nikko asked, faintly alarmed.

'Why, nothing! There's nothing to do. But don't worry, we'll pick up a bit of wind before long. Once the zenith is past, the wind will pick up again as the air cools. The only thing we'll have to worry about is making sure we don't get run down by a ship. Some of these foreign ships don't keep a very good lookout.'

They were becalmed, and Sally hove-to and they bobbed gently and aimlessly on a tranquil, sparkling water-bed.

'Let's have a swim,' Sally suggested. 'I could do with cooling off.'

'Okay, then. You go first.'

She stood up and pulled off her tee-shirt, and then sat down on the gunwale and swung herself neatly off into the water.

'Wow! It's cold!' she gasped, made breathless by the shock of the water. For a moment she hung on to the side of the boat, treading water and gasping, and then pushed herself off and swam ahead of the boat with long, slow strokes. Nikko took off his tee-shirt too, feeling the sun strike across his shoulders like a cymbal, and threw it with Sally's into the cabin out of the way. He watched her swimming, her brown body showing mysteriously white under the water, flickering lithe and firm like a fish's, all muscle. She swam without any splashing, like a dolphin; most people swim as though they're fighting the water, Nikko thought, but she just glides along with it. Now that's really what you'd call 'swimming like a fish'.

Sally came swimming back again, caught onto the gunwale, and hung there, treading with her feet and panting, looking up at Nikko with a dripping, smiling face.

'Give me a hand in,' she said. 'It's your turn now. It's absolutely delicious once you get used to the cold.'

'Do you know,' Nikko could not resist saying, 'that's exactly what I would have said about you.'

'What – oh!' Sally frowned with distaste. 'Very funny. Now give me a hand in, will you?'

With a writhe and a jump she got both her elbows up onto the gunwale, and hung there, waiting for him to help her. He crouched down and put his hands under her armpits and lifted, and with the help of her own wriggling she was soon over the side of the boat. But instead of letting her go, he pulled her closer to him, so that as he stood up she was pulled forward, held fast and unable to move. He hadn't really known what he was going to do – it was the work of a moment; but now she was pinioned against him, with her beautiful, furious face only an inch or so from his, he couldn't resist kissing her.

She resisted as well as she could, though he had her so tight she could hardly move at all, and when he released her she pulled away from him violently and stood glaring at him for a moment, her blue eyes brilliant and fierce as a siamese cat's. Nikko laughed, part triumphant, part uneasy.

'It's your own fault,' he said. 'You shouldn't look like that.'

'Like what?' she spat. She was so angry he thought sparks might fly out from her hair if he touched it.

'So cold and delicious,' he said, still laughing. Without a word she turned and went across to the other side of the boat. He didn't know what she was doing until too late – too late to save himself. Guided by her experienced hand, the boom swung across and hit his legs out from under him, so successfully that he made a perfectly curving flight over the side of the boat and hit the water, shoulder first.

The water felt icy, and the first shock made him gasp so that the salt sea ran into his open mouth and choked him. There followed a very bad three seconds before his head came up above the water again and he was able to spit out the water and take in some air instead. He floundered, gulping and gasping, for a minute, and then wiped the water out of his eyes and swam the few yards back to the boat. Sally stood safely inboard, watching him. Had she been laughing or challenging, it might not have ended there, but she was quiet and serious. He hooked himself onto the side of the boat, and she gave him a strong brown hand and hoisted him in, and gave him a towel.

'Don't do that again,' she said in a very matter-of-fact voice. He glanced at her sideways under cover of towelling his hair vigorously. She was wiping herself dry with another towel, and her hands were shaking, but when he saw from her face that she was still angry, he decided she was shaking from the effort of controlling her anger. He felt respect for her, and was sorry he had done it; but on the other hand he wanted to do it again, and add to it a sound slap for being so provoking. He was about to say the same, when she forestalled him by saying, 'We should have enough wind soon to get under way. I think we ought to have something to eat while we have the chance.'

'Okay,' he said, to make peace, 'I'll cook if you like. What'll it be? Baked beans?'

'Mm. They stick to your ribs all right.' She too was anxious for peace, and she smiled as she said, 'I'm starving. Put on some sausages too, and we'll have some beer to wash it down with.'

'Don't talk to me about washing it down – I've shipped about a gallon of sea water already,' Nikko said, making a joke of it.

'Never mind, it can't be harmful, or sailors would die young.'

They had sausages and beans, and a can of beer each, and by the time they were rinsing off the plates over the side, the breeze had got up and was flapping the loose bight of the sail gently.

'It'll serve,' Sally said, after snuffing and testing with a wetted finger. They got under way, and Sally consulted her compass again, and soon the pattern was re-established and they were running before the wind again. But now they did not speak, there was a tension between them, which neither of them could quite put a name to.

Once they were settled on course again, Sally said, 'We'd both better have a bit of a sleep, in case we're up late tonight. I'll go first. Just take the tiller, and keep us heading in the same direction. Here's my compass, look.'

'Like this?'

'That's right. Call me if the wind changes or if we come near anything, or if you need me for anything, and call me anyway at about four. Then you can go down and have a sleep. All right?'

'Yes, fine. Don't worry, I'll manage all right.'

'Keep a sharp lookout, won't you, for other ships?' Sally did not seem convinced of his capabilities.

'Yes, all right, don't worry. Go and have a snooze.'

Sally went down into the cabin and stretched herself out onto one of the bunks, covering herself with a blanket, not so much for the warmth as for the comfort, and went to sleep.

126

Nikko expected to be bored, but the time went past quickly, and he felt absolutely relaxed and happy, sitting holding the tiller and watching the sparkling water. Some cloud was building up in the west, but, though he was no weather expert, he didn't think it would reach them for a long time, perhaps not before dark. There was no land in sight anywhere, and no other ships, except one very distant on the eastern horizon; but he did not feel nervous or lonely. He felt very happy, very contented. I could stay here for ever, he thought.

Sally woke before he had to call her. He heard her washing her face and putting on some water to boil.

'I'll make some tea before I take over,' she called up to him.

'Good. I'm thirsty. It's getting chilly too – would you throw 's up a sweater?'

A little while later she came up on deck in jeans and tee-shirt, bringing the tea in mugs and a chunk – he was not polite enough to call it a slice – of bread and butter for them each. She checked the course, and then motioned him to hand over the tiller, and she settled herself on the transom with her mug in one hand, the tiller bar in the other, and her bare feet comfortably braced on the deck. The wind ruffled her hair a little, and her face was still a little flushed and sleepy, like a child's, from her nap.

'You look like a little girl,' he said.

She smiled a tranquil smile and said, 'Do I? I wonder why.'

He pretended to consider. 'I think it's your hair being tied up like that,' he said, but he was aware uncomfortably of his feelings for her growing more and more strong, and he said nothing more, but sipped his hot tea and looked at her over the rim of the mug as she stared out to sea, and glanced sometimes up at the leech of the sail.

'Go on down and have a sleep now,' she said at last, catching his eyes on her as she turned her head quickly.

'I don't really feel tired,' Nikko said.

'I don't expect you do, but you just lie down and you'll drop off before you know it.' She smiled kindly. 'Go on. I'll wake you in a couple of hours.'

127

Nikko went below and, having drained off his tea, did as she had done – he lay down on a bunk, and drew a blanket over him. At once the luxury of utter comfort spread like a warm glow all through him, and he felt so deliciously tired he could not have moved a limb even if they were sinking. He had time to register the thought that she was right before he fell without warning into a deep peaceful sleep.

CHAPTER FOURTEEN

When he woke, Nikko was aware at once that the movement of the boat had changed – it was jumpier, more irregular. He was aware also, a second or two after waking, that Sally had called him, and it was that which wakened him.

'Okay,' he called back to her. 'Coming.'

'Make some tea, will you,' she said.

He got up, and almost fell over again, as the new rhythm of the boat took him by surprise. He put the kettle on, washed his face, made the tea, and then as she had done before him, carried the tea up. He saw immediately that it was darker, for the sky had completely clouded over and brought on a premature dusk. The wind was fresher and the sea was choppy, and a small stirring of fear brushed the back of his neck.

'Are we in for a storm?' he asked her.

'Goodness, no. This is just a bit of cloud. We might get a spot of rain, but that's all. We'll have to go about soon, so get your tea down you.'

He came fully up on deck, and saw how the scene had changed while he slept. There were ships everywhere, of all shapes and sizes, all steaming along slowly in different directions – they were back in the main shipping lanes again. Ahead of them was the coastline, a dim grey smear along the horizon, bringing the horizon nearer in that direction. The water was no longer blue but a dirty grey, almost yellowish, making the blue sail look black with its negative reflection. Everything seemed suddenly cheerless, and he shivered.

'Cold?' Sally asked, in sympathy with him, it seemed, since his shiver had only been a tiny one.

'Not really. It's just waking up.'

'I know. You feel a bit wan at first, don't you?'

'Mm. So that's France,' he said, making conversation.

'That's France,' she agreed. 'We've made good time. I think we can put into St Martins for the night, which should save

129

trouble. I thought we might have to anchor somewhere down the coast and sail up there tomorrow.'

'I hope they've got a pub there,' Nikko joked.

'I sincerely doubt it,' she said calmly. 'I think the first signs of life we see we'll try and put in and get some food, and eat on board. Time enough for sightseeing tomorrow.'

'Well, you're the captain,' he said. 'We could get some wine as well, and do as the natives do.'

'Good idea,' she said. 'Finished your tea?'

They had to tack several times, dodging in and out of the big ships' paths. Once they passed a tanker so close they could hear the sound of music from one of the open portholes, and Nikko said, torturing himself, that he could smell cooking. They got close into the shore, and then the sailing became eventful, as they had to get close in to look out for houses and shops, and come out again when the water shoaled or a spit of rocks ran out into the sea. Nikko was glad of the activity, for waking to this changed world had left him with a kind of nightmare feeling, and he needed something to do to dispel it.

At last they came to a small inlet with a tiny piece of quayside and some lights shining in windows.

'This'll do,' Sally said. 'There's bound to be something here that we can buy. Get ready with the painter, mate.'

'Aye aye, Cap'n,' Nikko said, his spirits rising at the thought of dry land, food, and normality. Sally ran down the sails and steered in neatly, and together they caught hold of mooring lines and walked the Sea Wife along the wall to the harbour steps, where they tied up.

'Do you want to forage, or shall I?' Sally asked, Nikko's face fell.

'Can't we both go? I haven't given up hopes of a pub yet.'

'I don't think we should leave her. We don't know that we're allowed to stay here yet and somebody might come.'

'Oh, all right, I'll go, then. What shall I get.'

'Oh, just some bread and stuff. We've got some sausages left, but we could do with more milk if you can get any. Here, take some money.'

'French money eh – you think of everything!' Nikko exclaimed. He took a bag, and the money, put on his plimsolls, and scrambled up the steps. It was getting dark already. They wouldn't make St Martins, unless Sally intended to sail in the dark, and he wouldn't fancy that at all.

Sally had come to the same conclusion, and realized that they would have to stop there the night. Having made sure the ropes were secure, she too climbed up the steps and went in search of some authority of whom to request permission to moor. Further up the quay she came across two other boats moored, their sails furled, and on the deck of one of them was a prosperous-looking, middle-aged man with white hair, who looked as though he might be a company director on holiday.

She hailed him, and to her disappointment he turned out to be French, but when she made herself understood in a mixture of bad school French and wild gestures, he said he didn't see why she shouldn't tie up there, but don't ask him, he didn't know. No, he didn't know where the harbour master lived. He had never seen him. He had simply sailed in and moored, and no-one had troubled him. Not at all. He was mademoiselle's servant.

The man's shrug was catching, and with a large one, Sally made her way back to the Sea Wife and went below, to wait for Nikko to come back.

When he arrived she had already got sausages frying on one gas ring, and a mixture of milk and water heating on the other for cocoa, and the heat from the stove had made the cabin quite cosy. She had pulled the curtains across the two windows, and as he stood on the steps looking down, he felt quite pleased at the idea of spending the night on board, where before he had rather dreaded it.

'You look well settled,' Nikko said by way of announcing himself.

'Hello! How did you get on?' Sally asked. He came down into the cabin and with satisfaction closed the door behind him, shutting them in in the warmth and light.

'Okay, just about. I forgot people were likely to speak French, this being France, but it's amazing what a gesture or two will do.' He began to unload his bag. 'You were right, there isn't a pub, but I found a shop open and a very helpful old body presiding. I got onions – here, throw some in with the sausages – and bread – smells delicious – and some more eggs, and milk,' he placed each item on the table as he spoke, 'and some cheese, and garlic sausage – that's nearly singing to itself – and two bottles of wine. Bang Bang.'

'Well done, thou good and trusty servant,' Sally said, rapidly chopping onions in with the sausages. 'By gum, that garlic stick does smell, doesn't it? If I eat some, I'll have to make sure you eat some too.'

'And vice versa—'

' – or we won't be able to stand each other. The milk's just about to boil – put some cocoa into the mugs, will you. I didn't do all-milk; it's half and half. I wasn't sure you'd be able to get any, so I thought I'd better save a drop in case. But you can top it up with milk, now we've got plenty.'

'Rightyoh. Are those bangers nearly ready? – my stomach's just about touching my backbone.'

'Just about. Slap out a couple of plates. Shift that stuff into the lockers – come on, let the dog see the rabbit—'

'Patience, patience. Hang on, not the wine – we need that. Right.'

'Right.'

The sausages, brown and varnished, crackling gently as their crisp edges parted to let out a wisp of steam, were put onto the plates, and half covered by a steaming mound of fried onions, softly translucent, with one or two crisp tangy burnt ends. Nikko poured the milk into the mugs and stirred up the cocoa, while Sally cut chunks off the new French loaves and buttered them haphazardly, and then they both sat down, almost frantic with hunger, to eat.

Not a word was spoken until both plates and cups were empty, and then Nikko gave a sigh of satisfaction.

'Never in my life,' he said portentously, 'has anything tasted so good.'

'You said that about the sandwiches this morning,' Sally reminded him genially.

'It was true this morning. And it's true now.'

'Any spare corners left? Fancy a bit of garlic thingy and some wine?'

'Certainly to both. Let's be very French, our first night on French soil.'

'You aren't a whale on accuracy, are you?' Sally grinned.

'You kipper civil tongue in your head, my girl,' Nikko said.

'Ouch, what a pun!' Sally winced. 'Have you no sole?'

'You should learn to keep your plaice.'

'No more, no more, please. Have some wine. I give in.' Sally filled two cups hastily from the first bottle to hand, and pushed one over to Nikko. He lifted it, but paused before drinking and, smiling maliciously, said, 'There's a song that's very appropriate for this evening. Can you guess what it is?'

'I hate to think – all right, tell me.'

' "Salmon chanted evening." Cheers!'

Groaning quietly, Sally drank. The wine was rough, but good, a powerful young wine that would knock you over but not make you ill, and with it they ate slices of the garlic sausage on more chunks of bread.

'Have some more wine? This garlic thingy makes you thirsty, doesn't it?' Sally said.

'It's supposed to.'

'Why?'

'So you'll drink more wine. Cheers again!'

'Cheers. Why, do the wine-makers subsidize it, or something?'

'It's mutually beneficial. The garlic makes you thirsty, so you drink more wine; but if you drink more wine you have to eat or you get sick, so you eat bread; but bread's dull on its own, so you eat more garlic sausage.'

'So the bakers and vintners and – and – whatever garlic sausage makers are called – get richer and richer?'

'And the customers get drunker and drunker—'

'And fatter and fatter—'

'And happier and happier—'

'Are you happy?'

'Very. Aren't you?'

'Yes. I don't quite know why I should be, but I am,' Sally said, wondering a little.

'I can't think of any reason why you shouldn't be. Have some more wine.'

'I'd better not. I can't tell if it's me or if the boat's going up and down.'

'A little of both, I should think.'

'No, listen, I think the wind's getting up.' They listened for a moment in silence, and then Sally said, 'I'd better just go up and see that everything's secure, in case it does blow a bit during the night.'

'I'll come with you and hold the torch,' Nikko said gallantly.

'Thanks.'

It was almost quite dark outside now, and the air was fresh and keen, salty and more powerful than wine, and they took down great gulps of it, for the cabin had been stuffy, though they didn't notice it at the time. Nikko held the torch and shone it where she directed, while Sally stepped nimbly about the little craft, checking that everything was secure. It was blowing up a little, but not enough to worry about, though as they were standing there, enjoying the fresh air, there was a sudden flurry which tipped a capful of rain over them. Sally gave a convulsive shiver, and Nikko turned to look at her and smile, putting a hand to her cheek and saying, 'You're cold. Your face is like stone. Let's go back down.'

'Let's,' she said.

'We'll play a game of cards, or something, and finish off the wine, and then go to sleep.'

'As long as you don't cheat.'

'As if I would,' Nikko said, grinning at her. They went below into the light and the now-grateful warmth, and Sally got the cards out. The table when it was out for use was over one bunk, so they had to sit side by side on the other, and despite his protest, Nikko couldn't help cheating, because every time he looked at her he could see her cards.

'Well, don't look at me then,' Sally said indignantly, when he made this his excuse.

'Don't be silly, how can I help it?' he said, so frankly that she could hardly feel uncomfortable about it.

'I'll turn my back then,' she said, and played like that, shielding her cards with her body. She had to twist herself into a hairpin to be able to get her cards on the table, and in a moment she began to laugh, and then he started too, and in a minute or two they were too helpless with laughter to carry on playing.

'Oh dear, I give in. Let's say you've won,' Sally said, dropping her cards on the table and finishing off the wine in her cup. She was aware that she was a little drunk, but it was such a nice sort of drunk that she didn't mind, or feel ashamed. She just felt rosy and happy.

'That's not fair,' Nikko said. 'That takes all the pleasure out of winning.'

'You've won haven't you – what more do you want?'

'Two pin-falls and a submission,' he said.

'I'll never submit,' Sally said, waving a hand in the air.

'I know that,' Nikko said, putting his arms round her for the second time that day. 'We'll just call it an amalgamation.'

He kissed her, and she didn't object.

'Not a take-over bid?' she asked anxiously. He kissed her again.

'Not at all. I wouldn't do a thing like that to you.' He kissed her again.

'Oh good.' A pause. 'This is getting to be a habit.'

'Mm. Mind?'

'No.' Another pause. 'Only let's stop now, I'm falling asleep.'

'All right. After all, we've got all day tomorrow. And the next day.'

He looked into her sleepy, rosy face, and knew that he loved her, but at that moment it didn't worry him. They stood up and folded away the table, and then each got onto his own bunk, and drew up the blankets. Sally lay down at once and pillowed her cheek on her hand. Her eyes slid inexorably shut, and she smiled and said, 'Goo'night, Nick. Sweet dreams.'

Nick leaned up on one elbow to look at her, and he smiled too.

'Goodnight Sally.'

'Goo'night,' she murmured again, already half asleep. Nick reached up and turned off the gas lamp. He lay down in the darkness, and felt the boat moving gently under him.

'Goodnight, Sally, darling,' he said.

CHAPTER FIFTEEN

Sally woke very early the next morning, with a kind of holiday feeling, that something very exciting had happened, or was going to happen. For a moment she lay still, wondering where she was, and then the movement reminded her that she was on the boat, and she opened her eyes and saw the cabin in the grey light of early morning, and Nikko asleep a few feet away from her.

'Oh god,' she murmured, as full remembrance of the previous night came back to her. It was awful! Never mind that she had felt marvellous the night before; today was another day. What it boiled down to was, that she had got drunk and allowed him to kiss her – that was what it was, wasn't it? He would wake up in a minute and look at her and remember that she had got drunk and let him kiss her, and however would she be able to face him? Or herself, for that matter. She couldn't bear to look at him. She looked at the deck above and bit her lips to stop herself crying.

Whatever had possessed her to do such a thing? She hadn't felt drunk last night, but she knew she was. She had known it even then.

What was worse, she had enjoyed it. The idea shocked her, but then she told herself not to be silly – she must have found him pleasant to some degree, or she wouldn't have got him to accompany her on this trip. Naturally she had enjoyed it. There was nothing wrong in that.

No, what was so awful was the way it was done. When he had grabbed her, pulling her up on board after her swim, she had got so angry she had knocked him overboard; angry at his sheer cheek. Yet only hours later, she submitted to that same cheek, and why? – because she was drunk. Her cheeks flamed with shame. She had come on this boat to find out what had happened to Jim, not to conduct a romance with that insolent part-time reporter. She tried to think of Jim, but when she tried to fit his image together, all she could see was

Nikko's face as he had smiled at her just before he kissed her.

Well, that was the last time she drank wine like that. She might not be so lucky next time. She turned her face the other way and forced herself to look at Nikko as he lay sleeping peacefully in the other bunk. At first it made her blush, but she had to get through another day with him at close quarters, and she forced herself to look and look until the embarrassment faded away. He had very long eyelashes, she remarked, and his mouth was beautifully curved in relaxation.

By the time he woke, she was quite composed, and ready to face any kind of knowing remarks, or scornful looks he might give her; but he did none of these things. When he woke and saw her looking at him, he smiled a smile of pure pleasure, and murmured, 'Good morning.' Then he sat up, rubbing his face sleepily with his knuckles. 'I couldn't make out where I was at first. My, I do feel stiff.'

'I'll make some tea. You'll soon feel better. I expect you were bracing yourself against the roll during the night.'

'Could be. I'm just going up on deck for a minute.'

When he came back a few minutes later he looked fresher and better.

'It's misty and cold, but I think the sun's about to break through,' he said. 'You should go and have a look.'

'I will, as soon as I've got the kettle on.'

'Go on up – I'll do it.'

The little harbour was filled with mist like a bowl with milk, and it curled and sloshed gently around the stems of the other two boats moored up ahead of them. The air smelt marvellous, and there was a glimmering of light in the east which told that when the sun came up it would suck up all this mist and leave a hot perfect summer day. Distantly in the milky morning birds called, and herring gulls gave occasionally their unearthly cry. The water slapped and chuckled under the Sea Wife's keel, and the ropes creaked gently in chorus as she moved with the tide.

'It *is* lovely,' she said aloud.

'It is,' Nikko agreed from behind her, startling her.

'I didn't know you were so close,' she said. She avoided his eyes and said quickly, 'Let's get some breakfast on – I'm starving.'

For a moment it seemed as though he was going to say something, and Sally almost held her breath; but in the end he turned away and said in a cool, normal voice as he went down into the cabin, 'So am I. Let's have the full works. I make a pretty passable omelette.'

It was what she had wanted, but she felt an unreasonable small pang as he went, and had she known precisely what it was she thought he might have said, she might have called him back. As it was, she gave a shrug and went down after him.

They breakfasted on enormous cheese omelettes, bread and tea, which they ate sitting on the top step of the cabin where they could look out over the gunwales and watch the sun rising. It was chilly enough to make the hot tea and their thick sweaters grateful, but by the time they had finished eating and drinking it was warm enough to strip down to tee-shirts again. They would have lingered, it being such a perfectly lovely morning, but Sally was anxious to get away before anyone in authority turned up, in case they shouldn't have been there, and so they cleared away and sailed out of the little inlet before anyone was astir.

There was hardly any wind, even when they got into the open sea again, and they could just make way, tacking about every half-hour. In this way they spent an idyllic morning, basking in the sun, chatting lazily, drinking beer, as the Sea Wife drifted over a sea of blue and polished silver, like a shield.

Nikko didn't mention the events of the previous night, and Sally, gratefully, made no reference to it either; but the little activity and the idle chatter did nothing to take her mind off it, and often during that morning she found herself looking at Nikko, examining his face in minute detail as if she had never seen it before – which, in a sense, she never had. She did not really know what she thought or felt about him, except that she was surprised and grateful that he was being so restrained. He went up in her estimation for that.

They reached St Martins at about half past twelve. It was a

138

tiny place built on a river whose estuary was so silted up that at low tide there were only two narrow, shallow channels into the harbour. The harbour itself was much smaller than Pengarth's, and they could see at once that it was full of craft of all sizes.

'What's going on there? A regatta?' Nikko asked, shading his eyes to look.

'I don't know. Take the tiller a minute,' Sally said, and handing it over to him ran up onto the prow to look for herself. In a moment she was back to take over again.

'It's far too shallow to risk going in now,' she said. 'I don't say it couldn't be done, but I don't know the channels, and I'm not that good a sailor to want to risk it.'

'What then?'

'We'll have to hang around until the tide makes a bit. Let's see, high tide was around five this morning, wasn't it? That means the tide'll be turning now – I should think half an hour or so'll do it.'

'Maybe that's what all the boats are in there for – because they can't get out,' Nikko suggested. Sally snapped her fingers.

'You could well be right. It could be that they can only manoeuvre the channel at the full, in which case they would have come in with this morning's tide from last night's fishing, and be waiting to go out with this afternoon's.'

'Brains,' Nikko said, slapping his chest. 'Any little problem you have, just bring it to me.'

'Ass. Remind me when we get in to find a telephone and ring Gran. We should remember that, you know.'

'We should,' Nikko agreed. 'But the first priority will be food. I don't know why it should be, but I'm forever starving out here.'

They sailed cautiously into the harbour at around half past one, Sally with her heart in her mouth trying to visualize the shape of the sand banks as they had appeared above water an hour before. They touched once, but Nikko had the wit to throw himself across to the other side of the boat, and the Sea Wife rocked clear. They drifted up the harbour past the moored boats, and there was no-one to be seen – 'All having

139

their lunch I expect,' Nikko said. At last they found someone – a very old man with a nut-brown face and a white beard, sitting on deck mending a net. He was wearing, to Sally's delight, a black beret, and he looked the epitome of Frenchness.

He watched their approach with his eyes narrowed, and it was not until Sally actually caught onto his rubbing strake to hold the Sea Wife still that he put down his bone needle and came slowly across to speak to them. It took them a long time to get through to him, for he was somewhat deaf, it appeared, and besides he had probably never heard anything like their French. Certainly when he spoke to them his French was like nothing they had ever come across in a French Primer; but eventually they managed a modicum of mutual intelligence, and they gathered that it was all right for them to tie up anywhere beyond the line of bollards which marked the harbour proper where the fishing boats moored and unloaded.

'At least,' Sally said as she pushed them off again, 'I think that's what he said.'

'You mean you hope that's what he said,' Nikko grinned. 'Anyway, I can't see that we'll be in anyone's way here. If no-one's tied up now I can't see that they ever will.'

Driven by hunger they moored Sea Wife at the first available spot, made all secure, and scrambled ashore with their bag and money and headed for the main group of buildings. Nikko seemed to have an uncanny instinct for discovering shops, which wasn't as straightforward as it perhaps sounded, since the shops never looked like shops but simply like someone's back parlour, which they mostly were. The first place he nosed out seemed to be principally a butcher's shop, but Sally was horrified by the number of flies on the meat, and whispered as much to Nikko, who got them out with great dexterity and enquiries for the 'bureau de poste,' and a telephone, which is conveniently the same in almost every language. The old woman directed them copiously and followed them to the door, still talking. Sally could only catch about one word in four of what she said, but by now she had given up trying and was relying on Nikko's superior knowledge of the language.

'What was she saying?' she asked him when they were out of range.

'I didn't get it all, she spoke too fast, but I gather she thinks the post office will be closed because the woman has to get her man's lunch ready,' Nikko said.

'Had we better come back later?'

'Not at all. Even if she is getting her man's meal ready, she'll only be through the back of the shop.'

This proved to be true. The post office, which actually looked like a shop for a change, only like a grocery, not a post office, was shut, but another door directly next to it was open, and through the open door they saw a small, very dark woman planking plates and cutlery down onto a large kitchen table. She looked up as their shadows crossed the door, and an expression of apprehension crossed her face for a moment, before she hurried forward, wiping her hands on her apron and asking anxiously what they wanted.

Her face cleared with relief, so it seemed to Sally, when Nikko repeated their request for a telephone, and she hurried before them into the shop, which was not locked but merely closed, and pointed out the antique telephone apparatus.

Sally asked what coins were needed, and the woman got her change from the till, and then while Sally went back to telephone Nikko stayed with the woman in the back of the shop and engaged her in conversation.

The telephoning process was long, complicated, and frustrating. During the intervals when she was waiting for something to happen, Sally noted that Nikko was buying provisions; she saw money changing hands, and once the woman laughed, presumably at something Nikko had said. During another pause, however, she noticed to her amazement that they were talking rapidly and confidentially in a language that bore no resemblance to anything she had ever heard spoken – a queer, jerky, guttural kind of speech. She saw the woman shake her head hurriedly, as if denying something, and then listen again, frowning and biting her lip.

The next time Sally looked round, she saw money passing across again, at what was apparently the end of the conversation, for immediately Nikko walked away to stand in the doorway, waiting for her, while the woman disappeared through a door in the back of the shop.

'Any luck?' Nikko asked when the woman had gone.

'Not really. All I've got is what sounds like a pound of sausages frying. I think I might as well give it up.'

'Well, it *was* a little ambitious to expect to get through to a tiny English village from a tinier French one,' Nikko said, smiling.

'Maybe you're right,' Sally said, and replaced the receiver with a sigh. 'Have you got everything?'

'I have now,' Nikko said, turning with a smile as the woman came back with two bottles of wine. 'Merci beaucoup, madame,' he said, taking them from her.

'Merci, m'sieur. Mademoiselle n'a pas de chance?'

'Pas du tout. Ça ne fait rien. A bientôt.'

'Au 'voir M'sieur.' Nikko pushed one of the bottles into Sally's arms and steered her briskly out of the door, and the woman hurried after them and into her own house with what looked like relief. Sally stared up at Nikko's face, and he was smiling smugly.

'What on earth—' she began, but he grinned down at her and said, 'Not a word until we're back on board.'

Sally shrugged. If that was the way he wanted it – 'Did you get everything?'

'I got the ingredients of a meal at any rate.'

'And all this wine—'

'Well, the intention is not to drink it all at once this time,' Nikko said, grinning wickedly at her. He was certainly in high spirits. 'Though of course, if you insist on leading me astray . . .'

'Why, you beast, of all the rotten things to say.'

'Hush, little one, it's only a joke.'

'It doesn't make me laugh.'

'Hush, or I shan't tell you.'

Back on the Sea Wife they hurried below and put down their purchases, and then Sally turned firmly to Nikko, arms akimbo, and said, '*Now* tell me. What was that funny language you were talking to her?'

Nikko gave a triumphant grin. 'That funny language, as

you call it with a cheek that wants beating out of you, was Romany.'

'Romany?' Surprise and doubt were in equal proportions in her expression.

'Yes. I thought she might be Romany by the look of her, so while she was off guard I asked if she janned the can—'

'If she what?'

'Janned the can – slang for spoke Romany – and immediately her face lit up and she started jabbering away as if she'd known me all her life.'

'And did you find out anything?' Sally asked eagerly, not caring too much about all this gypsy nonsense.

Her expression must have shown as much, for Nikko looked at her rather oddly, and said, 'Romany people stick together, you know. They're very clannish, and while they'll fleece any gayjo they can lay palms on, they'll do almost anything to help another of their own sort. You should remember that, and not be so sceptical.'

Sally knew what he was getting at, and looked a little shamed.

'All right – I'm sorry. But what did you find out?'

'It wasn't all that easy,' Nikko said, picking up one of the bottles of wine and starting to open it. 'First of all I thought I'd just lay my cards on the table, but a natural caution made me go slowly and watch her reactions. I told her that you were an English girl looking for your man, and when I saw the sneer on her face, I added that you were a rich English girl, and gave her a wink, and let her think what she liked.' Sally's expression made him laugh, and he said, 'Sorry if you don't like it, but I had to keep her on my side. Well, then I said that there was money in it for me if I could find the man, and that I knew he had been brought to this part of the coast by smugglers.'

He had the bottle open now, and paused to take a mouthful before continuing.

'When I said that – I didn't know the word for smugglers, and I had to talk round it a bit – she kind of shook her head, as if she was trying to say there weren't any smugglers in these parts, but she did it too quickly, and I could see she

143

was worried. Then I thought it was probably because her own man was one of them.'

'Really? Do you think so?' Sally, in her excitement, took the bottle from Nikko without noticing, and took a swig of the wine in her turn.

'It was a kind of stab in the dark, but I had nothing to lose. I went on a bit and then I looked her straight in the eye and said that if the English girl didn't find out something, she might get the police in on the search. "Now you wouldn't like that, would you?" I said.'

'You're taking a chance,' Sally said mildly. 'Supposing she calls out her husband and his cronies – we might get lynched.'

'Not likely – all they want to do is avoid trouble, and Romanies don't like the police any more than smugglers do. Anyway, even if it was a risk, it paid off.'

'Why? What did she say?'

'She said she had heard something about the man, but she knew very little. She said she would find out something more, and I was to come to the end of the jetty after the boats had gone out and she would tell me what she had found out.'

'This is fine! Now we're really getting somewhere. Which end of the jetty have we got to meet her?'

'We? Are you coming then? Not afraid of lynching?'

'Why should I be? I've got a real live Romany gypsy to protect me,' Sally said.

CHAPTER SIXTEEN

The woman was waiting when they got to the appointed place. She was wearing a light shawl with the end folded round her head, like the Irishwomen in old prints, and she looked very furtive. As it was still broad daylight, Sally felt a strong desire to giggle, but then restrained herself, thinking that the woman was probably scared stiff that her husband would find out and beat her up – presumably that kind of thing went on on both sides of the Channel.

The three of them stood in a huddle, but the woman spoke only to Nikko. The conversation was brief and terse, and the exchange went on entirely in Romany, so it did Sally no good at all being there, except that she wouldn't have missed any part of this human treasure-hunt. Once during the exchanges the woman looked briefly at Sally, and a glint of dislike – almost hatred – flashed from the brown eyes to the blue. Then the talk was all over, Nikko gave her money, and the group split up.

'Well, that was all very efficient,' Sally said coldly. 'And what did she say this time? Apart from laying a curse on me?'

'Oh, don't worry about that,' Nikko said lightly. 'No woman ever likes another woman better-looking than her. She's found out what we want, anyway, on the gypsies' grapevine, but we'll have to get away quickly, before the tide drops too far and we're trapped.'

'Get away where?'

'To Deux Eglises. That's where the story is,' Nikko said, dropping into reporter's language without really meaning to. 'Her brother who plies the roads between here and there has discovered that the foreign sailor who was picked up that night was brought into Deux Eglises. He was taken to the house of an old woman called Simonette to be nursed. She has arranged, through her brother, that we should meet

Simonette at around ten tonight by the last boathouse on the left-hand quay.'

'We really had better hurry, then,' Sally said eagerly, quickening her pace towards the Sea Wife, but Nikko caught her arm just above the elbow and pulled her round to face him. He looked at her with an expression of concern and a rather puzzled sympathy, that made her pulses beat a little more quickly just for a moment.

'Sally – listen – don't expect too much, will you?' He searched her face earnestly. 'I mean – you know he can't be alive, don't you?'

Their eyes held for a painful moment, before Sally lowered hers, and said in a subdued voice, 'I know, Nick. Don't worry.' She glanced up again. 'I just want an end now.'

'Okay. Come on then, let's go.'

The tide took them out comfortably and they sailed round the coast on the strong land-breeze which, though it necessitated constant tacking, was a good deal better than the paltry little winds they had experienced before. They made Deux Eglises around nine, but they stood off a fair distance as there were still craft coming out for the night's fishing – or whatever they were going to be doing that night – and they didn't much want to get involved with any of them.

Deux Eglises' harbour was entirely different from St Martins' – no sandbanks, no mud tie-ups, just a small, thriving harbour surrounded on three sides with proper quays and warehouses, and a narrow entrance already showing its lights. When they went in the harbour was empty but for one old hulk tied up and apparently rotting in the farthest corner, and a couple of prams tied to rings in the quayside.

'Plenty of choice,' Nikko commented. 'Where shall we go?'

'Somewhere we can make a quick getaway, in case your Romany friend isn't all you think she is,' Sally said. The gloom of the twilight made her nervous.

'Don't be an ass. This is the twentieth century. It's smugglers we're dealing with, not pirates,' Nikko said.

'All the same, I don't want to risk the boat. We'll tie up over there. The way the tide makes we'll be able to get straight out from there.'

'As you please,' Nikko shrugged. 'We'll have time for a meal, anyway, before the big appointment.'

They tied up in the place Sally had chosen, about fifty yards from the boathouses beyond which they were to meet the old woman called Simonette, and cooked a meal, but Sally could not eat from nervousness. Nikko tried to get her to take some wine, but she wouldn't, and made herself some tea instead, which she drank, saying she was thirsty. Nikko refused the tea and drank the wine himself.

'Needing Dutch courage?' Sally asked rather nastily, but he wasn't to be baited.

'You should have seen me the night I went off to speak to your Frenchy Polwhatsit,' he said cheerfully.

'And you never did speak to him in the end, did you?'

'Nope. And I'm proud of it. If you can collect crocodile's teeth without putting your hand in the crocodile's mouth, are you cowardly or merely very clever?'

Sally grinned unwillingly. 'I hope this Simonette character doesn't speak Romany too – I'd like to get in on some of the action.'

'I hope she does,' Nikko countered promptly. 'I've a better chance of telling if she's telling the truth if it's in a language I know.'

'Do you think she might lie? Why?'

'For the money of course, infant.'

'Oh. I hadn't thought of that. Still, we can show her the photo, see if she recognizes it.'

'What photo?'

'The photo of Jim I brought along,' Sally said.

Nikko's face lit up into a smile, and he took Sally's face between his hands and said solemnly, 'You brought a photo! Sally, what a clever girl you are. I could kiss you!'

'Of course, she might pretend to recognize it,' Sally said with difficulty, her cheeks being all out of shape between Nikko's hands, not quite knowing if she wanted him to kiss her or not. Nikko seemed to recognize the indecision in her eyes and released her quickly.

'Of course, she might. But it's usually easy enough to tell

147

if a person really recognizes a photo or if they're pretending. They—'

'Sshh! What's that?' They froze. 'Someone outside,' Sally whispered. Nikko crept up to the steps, and at the same moment the boat rocked as someone stepped on board. For a moment Sally quivered with fear, but almost immediately a figure appeared openly at the open cabin door, looking at them without any suggestion of menace or furtiveness.

'I am Martha's brother,' he said in English, but with a thick, almost guttural, accent. Then he picked out Nikko, and continued in Romany, a brief sentence. Nikko turned to Sally to translate.

'He said he's come to take us to Simonette.' The man apparently followed what Nikko said, because he pointed one gnarled, oil-blackened finger at Nikko, and then at Sally, and said, again in English 'I take. You, yes. But no English. No gayjo.' His eyes, almost invisible in his brown-black face under their bushy eyebrows, glinted at Sally so that she felt another, similar, quiver of fear.

'What does gayjo mean?' she asked Nikko, to cover for herself.

'It's a rather rude word meaning "foreigner",' he said, with a light grin. 'I suppose you could roughly translate it as "wog".'

'Oh, I see.' Sally looked doubtfully, first at Nikko, then at the man.

'I'll have to leave you alone for a while, then, Sally. Do you mind?'

'No, I suppose not. There's no-one around anyway,' she said with a courage she didn't feel.

'Look,' Nikko said, 'if you feel really nervous, put off and sail about for a bit.'

'In the dark? Single handed?' Sally said derisively.

'Well, all right, row out to that mooring buoy out there and wait for me. I'll take the torch and signal when I want to come back, and you can row back for me.'

'All right. Off you go then.'

'I'll be as quick as I can.'

148

'All right. Wait! – don't you want the photo?'

'Yes, of course, silly of me. And the torch, of course. Right, now I'm off.'

Nikko followed the swarthy man up onto the quayside, and Sally, feeling as much foolish as afraid, hauled out the heavy oars and pushed the Sea Wife away from the quay and towards the buoy.

The man Nikko followed along the darkening quay was one of the swarthiest, dirtiest, darkest men he had ever seen, but he felt no fear of him. He was one of Nikko's own kind, and their common language made Nikko feel safer with him, almost, than he felt with ordinary English people.

There was a dark shadow waiting at the end of the line of boathouses, where the clayey cliff came down in a slide to meet the harbour, and as they came nearer the shadow detached itself and proved to be a small and shrivelled old woman dressed like a Greek widow in black, long black skirt, black shawl, and a black scarf round her head. Her face was bony and hawklike under the wrinkled brown skin, and her eyes, though beginning to be milky, were large and well-shaped. She must have been a beauty in her youth, he thought.

'Here is the man who wishes to know about the foreign sailor,' the man said to Simonette in French, and then, turning to Nikko, said, 'She does not have the English, nor the Speech. You must talk to her in French.' Then he retired a pace like a referee at a boxing match and watched them, while Simonette and Nikko sized each other up. Nikko spoke first, in French as directed, and all their conversation was carried on in that tongue.

'Well, mother,' he said. 'One has said to me that you nursed the foreign sailor on the night of the storm.'

'Ah, that was a mighty storm,' she said evasively. 'A storm such as we had when I was a child and this harbour was no more than a few huts and a wooden jetty. Then the storms used to take off the roofs of the houses, and kill the seabirds in their hundreds.'

'It was a mighty storm,' Nikko agreed patiently, 'and it killed many men. One of them was brought here, to this village, and to your house. What did he look like, mother?'

'A tall man, he was, and strong. It took two big men to carry him.' She gave a smile like a tiger licking its lips, and said, 'He had strong arms, and smooth skin. A boy, just in manhood, a man with fair hair like a boy.'

Well I'll be damned, thought Nikko to himself. The lascivious old bitch.

'Was he dead, mother?'

'No, no, not dead. For what would they have brought me a dead sailor?'

'He was near to death,' the man broke in at that point. 'He was half drowned, and frozen cold. He was unconscious.'

Old Simonette seemed to resent having her story taken from her and told so briefly, and she flashed the man a look of resentment and said, 'He was close to death, yes, but not dead. They carried him into my house and laid him on the bed that was my son's before the sea took him.' She crossed herself piously.

'Did the man speak to you? Did he say anything?'

'He was unconscious for a long time, many hours, while I dried and warmed him. Then he woke, and spoke to me.'

'What did he say?' Nikko managed to restrain himself just in time from shouting in his excitement. The tension of the hunt had got to him at last. But the old woman merely shrugged.

'How would I know what he said? He spoke in his own tongue. I do not speak foreign tongues.'

'Was no-one else there? Did no-one else hear?' Nikko asked in a last hope.

'No-one else could spare the time to be with the foreign sailor. That was why they brought him to me to nurse. I nursed him all through the night, and I thought that he would recover, for he was young and strong, but he did not. He died in the morning when the tide turned.' Her regret was strong in her voice.

He had expected that. He had not expected him to be alive, and so was not disappointed. But there was just the test now – he pulled out the photograph.

'Now, mother, I am glad of your news. Just look at this picture, will you, and say if it is the man you nursed.'

'My eyes are poor, and the light is poor,' Simonette complained as she took the photograph.

Nikko stood beside her and directed his torch onto the picture, and she turned it this way and that and peered at it with her head tilted back. Then at last she sighed and said, 'It may be the man, it could be. He was this age, and his hair was fair – but – my eyes are poor, and I cannot be sure. No, I cannot be sure.'

She passed the picture back, regretfully, her fingers loath to let it go, and Nikko took it and pocketed it, well pleased. This proved she was honest, for if she had been making the story up for the sake of the money, she would have said that it was definitely the man. He felt in his pocket for money, and slid it into her hand.

'You have told me much, mother, and I am grateful. If you will just tell me now—'

'But are you not wanting the papers?' the man blurted out. Simonette and Nikko looked at him, and then at each other, and Simonette shrugged.

'The papers that I took out of the young man's pockets. Perhaps you would like to see them?'

'But of course!' Again Nikko nearly shouted, with impatience this time. He had not thought of papers surviving. He held out a hand that trembled with excitement as Simonette fumbled in the folds of her clothes for some hidden pocket, and came out with what looked like a letter, folded up, and a small, thin green book with a fabric cover, about the size and shape of a driving licence, which she passed unwillingly across to him.

The paper was stiff and lumpy, as paper is that has been soaked and dried, and from the ink smears on the outside he doubted if it would be legible. He slid it unexamined to the bottom and looked first at the green booklet. It had nothing at all printed on the outside, but its covers were stiff card under fabric, and he had better hopes of its contents. He opened it. The writing that had been filled in in ink was

151

hopelessly smeared, but the printing was undamaged. It was an identity card of some sort, and it was printed in what Nikko recognized, even with his limited knowledge, unhesitatingly as Swedish.

The foreign sailor had not been Jim at all, but one of the shipwrecked Swedes from the cargo ship.

CHAPTER SEVENTEEN

For a long moment he stood staring down at the card, all the excitement drained from his face, and bitterness twisting his mouth.

A Swedish sailor, not Jim at all. Now the whole pointless search would begin again, and Sally would go on eating her heart out over this senseless, stupid . . .

No wonder the old woman didn't recognize the picture! And of course, since she didn't speak any other languages, she wouldn't have known if he was talking English or Swedish – it would have been all the same to her!

Simonette and the man had been watching him all the time, and when at last he looked up and met their eyes, they looked sad and sympathetic.

'It isn't the man monsieur is seeking?' the man said gently.

'No. It isn't the man,' Nikko said in a flat voice. 'All this way, all this time for nothing!' He made a gesture of anger, but caught himself up suddenly as an idea came to him – perhaps it was not for nothing after all!

'Wait,' he said, 'listen.' The man, who had been looking rather worried, no doubt on account of his worry for his sister should the mad English girl call in the police to search for this missing man, brightened at the change in Nikko's expression. 'Listen,' Nikko said, 'I have an idea. The English girl wants to know what happened to her man. She will not rest until she knows the worst, and until she rests, I cannot rest – understand?'

The man nodded solemnly, but old Simonette gave a ghostly chuckle.

'I understand, monsieur. Yes, yes, I understand.' And she laughed again.

You've got an evil mind, you old harridan, Nikko said silently, and then went on aloud, 'If I brought the girl here, would you tell her all that you have told me, excepting only

153

that you took papers from his pockets? If she sees these papers, she will know it is not the man, but otherwise—' He gave a very French shrug.

'But of course. I will do this for you,' Simonette said, her hand twitching out automatically.

'And one other thing – she is bound to want to know where he is buried. Can you show us the place?'

Simonette looked doubtful. 'Monsieur, it was a body we did not want and could not explain—'

'What did you do with it?'

'The sea, monsieur. It was dropped into the sea.'

'Oh.' There was a pause, and then the man broke in again with some eagerness in his voice – he was caught up in the conspiracy too, it seemed.

'There is an unmarked grave, behind the old church, which is now ruined since the war. It is not far.'

Nikko snapped his fingers. 'I'll go fetch her. Just say what you have said to me – oh, and when I show you the picture, say that this is definitely the person.'

'Don't worry, monsieur. We shall do as you say.'

Nikko would have laid a bet that they were attributing him with motives of the utmost greed and callousness in wanting to deceive Sally in this way, but in fact it was quite the reverse, though he would never be able to mention it to anyone. The identity card he would send back to the Swedish authority concerned with an anonymous note. The letter, which he examined as he hurried back along the jetty, was quite indecipherable, and he tossed it into the water, and slid the i.d. card into the depths of his side pocket.

Poor Sally! It would be a shock to her to have confirmed at last what she had dreaded all along, but it was for the best, and he believed she had spoken truly when she said she only wanted an end now. He didn't believe she still loved or longed for Jim, and once the mystery and doubt about him was resolved, Nikko was convinced that she would lay his memory to rest, and be ready to start afresh. With a clean slate. On which he could write? – well, perhaps. Why not? Nikko liked to hedge to himself, for his freedom was a precious thing to him, but he knew that he loved Sally as he probably would never love anyone else, and even if he failed to win her, he would never stop loving her.

But he didn't think for a minute that he wouldn't win her, and he smiled as he signalled her to come in for him, smiled with pleasant anticipation. Then he straightened his face and put on an aspect of respectable gloom as the shape of the boat loomed up out of the dark.

He caught the painter as she tossed it to him, and made the boat fast, and then stepped down on board and, confronting Sally, took both her hands in his. They were warm from the rowing, and his were cold.

'Well? Did you find out?' she asked, her voice fevered with anxiety. He could not see her face in the darkness, but he knew it too well not to know what was its expression, and with the image in his mind of the face he loved, the lie came out easily.

'Yes. I found out. It was him.' She gave a little shuddering sigh, and he felt her relax suddenly. He reached out and drew her towards him, and she came without a struggle and allowed him to cradle her in his arms for a moment. Then he said, 'She's waiting up there. She will tell you the story herself, from her own lips, and show you the grave.'

'I don't think I want—' Sally began, but Nikko interrupted firmly.

'Yes, you do. You must finish it now you've begun it, so that you have no room for doubts or accusations afterwards. You have to go through with it now, Sally.'

'Yes, I suppose I do. Come, then, let's go.'

It was over quite quickly, and without much speech. Simonette told the story again, briefly, and Sally asked a question or two, equally briefly, in her schoolroom French. Then there was the short walk through the darkness to the ruined church, and they stood by the unmarked grave in silence for a moment. Sally looked at the grassy mound, and then at Simonette.

'He is really dead, then?' And the question was hardly addressed to the old woman, but to herself in wonder – she could hardly take it in.

'Yes, mademoiselle. I saw him die. When the tide turned and began to ebb, he died. That is how sailors die.'

'Thank you for telling me, madame,' Sally said, slowly. Then she turned her face to Nikko. The moon was rising, and by its light he could see her face, and the expression of lightness, almost of amusement, that was on it.

'Let's go, Nick. Now it's all over, I just want to get home as soon as possible.'

'We can't sail until dawn,' he said.

'No, but we can get everything ready, and then get a little sleep, and be off at first light. I don't want to waste a minute.'

'Just as you like. I thought you might like to have a look round, do a bit of touristing.'

Sally shook her head, and gave a little shudder.

'No. I've seen nothing but two little fishing villages, but somehow that's as much as I want to see. I don't think I'll ever come back to France.'

'Poor France,' Nikko teased gently.

'I don't expect it will mind,' she said gently.

In the first, faint, grey light they set sail from the small harbour, and watched the sun rise in pink and gold glory as they headed back up the Channel towards Ushant, where they would turn and head across towards England. Nikko ought to have been happy at this satisfactory conclusion, but somehow the nearer they got to home, the more ill at ease he felt. How was he going to maintain his relationship with Sally now that they had no common goal to work for? He could not afford to live at the hotel much longer, and what excuse could he produce for hanging round her anyway?

And apart from anything else, there was this mood of Sally's: he had expected her to be more peaceful, happier – that was why he had done it – but she passed from being amused to being positively gleeful, and he didn't understand it.

The climax came when they were becalmed temporarily out in mid-Channel. Nikko suggested swimming, but Sally felt too warm and idle and suggested instead they drink their last two cans of beer and just dabble their feet. He agreed, and it was in this lazy, relaxed posture that Sally exploded her bombshell under his feet.

'I wonder,' she said idly, 'what really happened to him?'

'To whom?'

'To Jim, of course. Now, Nick, don't look so startled – you didn't really think I believed all that, did you?'

He was too startled and embarrassed to say anything, but she smiled at him kindly and said, 'That grave, you see – it was far more than a year old. The grass was tough and well-rooted, and there was no sign of sinking. And then I couldn't see why they would have bothered to bury him at all – far more likely they would just have dumped him at sea, rather than risk carting him through the streets at night and burying him in secret in a deserted churchyard – it didn't make sense.'

Nikko cleared his throat, but found nothing to say. He could not meet her searching eye, and looked out to sea blankly.

'And then, you know, she recognized him far too definitely from the photo. It wasn't a very clear photo, and her eyes didn't look any too good.'

'Sally—' Nikko began, but she put a hand on his wrist, a cold hand, which she had been dabbling in the water, on his hot wrist, which had been toasting in the sun.

'No need to perjure yourself, Nick. The sailor's card fell out of your pocket when we gybed this morning. I know who it was – well, as much as you do, anyway.'

She slid the little green card across to him with the tips of her fingers, and he took it without looking at it and put it back into his treacherous pocket.

She ran her fingers down from his wrist to his hand, and curled her fingers around his. They had a friendly feel, but they made him shake all the same. She said, 'I know why you did it, Nick, and I'm grateful to you. You were quite right. It came to me when I looked at that grave. I saw that it wasn't Jim's grave, and then I thought to myself, what difference would it have made what grave they showed me? It would have been all the same. I knew then that he really was dead, and I didn't need anyone to show me the evidence. I accepted it.'

Nikko nodded sympathetically, not daring to speak because of the lump in his throat.

'I made up a big mystery where there was none. I couldn't face up to things, and so I invented stories for myself, like an orphan telling itself stories about how its mother and father were a king and queen and how the gypsies stole it when it was a baby – you know what I mean?'

'Yes,' said Nikko.

'I've been very silly and childish about the whole thing, but you've cured me, and I'm very grateful. I hope you forgive me for wasting all your time and effort. And money – you must have paid her a fortune! But it did the trick, and I am grateful, Nick.'

'Sally, I don't want gratitude,' Nikko began with an effort.

'No?' she said innocently, so innocently, with a mocking smile lurking in the background that he wanted to throttle her and kiss her all at once. Kiss her most, though.

'You know, don't you,' he blurted out, 'that I love you?' That wasn't very suave, he told himself crossly – but then he wasn't feeling suave; just in love. Sally looked at him for a long moment, and then the mockery died out of her face, leaving a smile of lovely serenity.

'Yes, I suppose I do.'

'Do you mind?'

She didn't speak this time, just shook her head, her eyes shining and her mouth closed and smiling. He put an arm round her hesitantly, and then the other too, and drew her gently to him, and they exchanged the first of many kisses as the Sea Wife bobbed and dipped gently on the sapphire sea.

And presently, though they didn't heed it at first, they felt the gentle stirring of the air around their faces as the wind revived that was to take them home.